Whispers in the Wind

RITA DUNHAM

Gotham Books

30 N Gould St.
Ste. 20820, Sheridan, WY 82801
https://gothambooksinc.com/

Phone: 1 (307) 464-7800

© 2023 *Rita Dunham*. All rights reserved.

No part of this book may be reproduced, stored in a retrieval system, or transmitted by any means without the written permission of the author.

Published by Gotham Books (September 27, 2023)

ISBN: 979-8-88775-449-9 (P)
ISBN: 979-8-88775-450-5 (E)

Because of the dynamic nature of the Internet, any web addresses or links contained in this book may have changed since publication and may no longer be valid.

The views expressed in this work are solely those of the author and do not necessarily reflect the views of the publisher, and the publisher hereby disclaims any responsibility for them.

TABLE OF CONTENTS

CHAPTER 1 1
CHAPTER 2 18
CHAPTER 3 27
CHAPTER 4 44
CHAPTER 5 72
CHAPTER 6 81
CHAPTER 7 95
CHAPTER 8 103
CHAPTER 9 117
CHAPTER 10 128
CHAPTER 11 138
CHAPTER 12 151
CHAPTER 13 165
CHAPTER 14 173
CHAPTER 15 186
CHAPTER 16 194

Chapter 1

Vicky could feel the vicious sting of her adversary's evil stares. The hatred in her eyes, piercing through her soul, all the way from across the room. Sharp enough to penetrate bone. She was zoning in... Watching...Waiting. Soaking up each and every movement from a distance as she contemplated on the right moment to strike. Animosity so blatant it had to be a crime, especially without reasonable or probable cause. It was definitely war without conviction.

Where it all came from she would never know - but the rivers from which it flowed ran boundless and deep. Disdain so deep she couldn't have ignored it even if she had tried. Yet every single day she had to cope with it. Deal with this knucklehead as if she didn't exist, eventhough her antics were bold as daylight. It was the true definition of utter insanity at its best. Pure torture. And every day that she kept her distance was a *good* day to say the least. Afterall, the more "space" the merrier. Vicky cringed as her mind recaptured all of the emotional trauma she had endured... the pain and suffering under the vicious reign of her nemesis as pangs of helplessness kicked up in the pit of her stomach, churning like a raging storm.

She had neither the time, desire nor inclination to even attempt reconciling with a possibly insane person. Her main goal and focus was to get out of dodge with her mind still intact, if at all possible. Though deep down in her heart of hearts, she knew all too well the depths of Carlotta's fixation to bring her down and that she would stoop to any level to accomplish her objective. Use any and everything in her power to make leaving as difficult and as humanly incomprehensible as she could - if not finding a way to totally destroy her altogether... nothing was beneath her. But she still had to try for the sake of her mental, despite the insatiable wiles of her adversary. Her sanity. No matter how she tried to manipulate and control her, she was not going down without a fight. She knew Carlotta had peeped her weaknesses, but she also knew her strength. And she knew the only possibility of maintaining the upperhand was to victimize her. To keep her oppressed and in bondage. Aggravated and stagnated. But in order to weild that type of power she had to keep her close. She needed access and control, being the nutjob that she was. But being underestimated was a powerful tool, if used properly. And because of her arrogance, the left hand had been exposed to the right. Now her back door was open.

Vicky stared out the window in deep thought, reminiscing about the days of freedom as she held back the tears. Striving to maintain her composure under the scrutinizing glare of her rival. She *had* to escape. But how? Leaving a homeless shelter wasn't easy... if not next to impossible. All she ever wanted was to be left alone. She had done nothing to no one. Nothing to warrant such malice and disapproval... Played it safe her whole entire life. Staying in her lane. Playing her position. She didn't come from the streets and had no intention of perpetrating. Just doing her own thing like everybody else, until she finally got out... away from it all.

She owed nothing to nobody and definitely wasn't about to be victimized by Carlotta or anybody who even looked like her, for that matter. Vicky sucked it up, refusing to bow under the persecution as she weaved through the brazen stares and headed toward the food counter amidst the whispers, then took her place in line just before the lights went out. Overtaken by the sudden jolt of gravity she met the hard surface of the floor... then quickly sprung forward, skillfully maneuvering a fistful of the silky cloth clutched between her fingers, Vicky leveled her opponent to the ground.

"*Try me...*" She whispered, gathering a clump of the mangled ponytail. A blur of lights flashing before her in a whir of confusion as her chin collided with the back of Carlotta's head... floating in and out of consciousness.

"Hold her down!" A loud voice rose from the rowdy crowd of women as a circle formed in a sea of clapping hands and shouts fueling the altercation as Vicky slowly pulled forward, trying to rationalize...make sense of the whole thing, she slammed backwards and rolled to the side as she felt herself slowly slipping away.

*****

It had been three unforgiving hours since it all went down as she slowly opened her eyes and looked around the room at the old school clock on the wall, then eased up from the cot and made her way across the room. The stitches were still fresh and sore to the touch as she examined her face in the bathroom mirror. The dark marks around her eyes had swollen to tiny slits as she squinted to see the faucet, then quickly turned it on dousing her face with water before heading back to the day room toward the soup line.

"Got a light?" The fair-skinned short stocky woman with bright pink locks glanced over her shoulder.

"Sorry, I don't smoke." Vicky massaged her throbbing temples and adjusted her eye glasses, smoothing back her hair checking the neat little bun in the back of her head was still in place.

"I'm Carlotta and you are?"

"Vicky." She leaned against the wall to steady herself.

"You can go." The woman stepped to the side motioning her to the front of the line.

"I got you next time." Vicky took her place.

"You good. Hey, that was quite a nasty little scuffle you had yourself earlier, you okay?"

"Not exactly." Vicky closed her eyes for a moment, bracing against another dizzy spell, then stepped forward as she fought back the tears.

"You really oughta get something cold on that right away." Carlotta reached for a styrofoam cup on the counter and pressed the lever on the machine filling it with ice, then handed it to her.

"Thanks." Vicky reached for the cup and placed it against her blackened eyes.

"Hey, no problem... I take it you're not one of her favorites..."

"Probably not."

"So what gives?"

"I truly have no idea, but that's an excellent question." She transferred the homemade cold pack to the other eye. "All I can say is it's the gift that just keeps on giving... and hopefully one day I can give it all back."

"Now that's a good one. Laugh out loud. I gotta admit I do dig your sense of humor, although I'm not so sure I'd be joking if it were me and I had just gotten side swiped like that, especially out of nowhere... just sayin'."

"I feel you." Vicky quickly examined the room, careful not to get snaked again. "Getting stole on is never an easy thing to deal with, I'd have to agree."

"I believe you. So what exactly brings you to this hell-hole anyway, if you don't mind me asking."

"In a nutshell??? LIFE."

"Cause you most definitely don't look like you belong here."

"Trust, I most definitely don't feel like I belong here, neither. That's for sure."

"Hey, I wouldn't either if I was you. Especially if I just got my head peeled - and for no apparent reason, might I add."

"Precisely."

"Word to the wise though, the one you just ran up on? That Anita person? She a real work of art. A real *Chicago Finest*, if you know what I mean. The elevator don't always rise to the top floor if you get my drift. It's like the luck of the draw with her."

"Thanks for the heads-up."

"Not a problem. You really gotta watch your back around here so don't get too comfortable, you can't afford to get too laid back. Because trust and believe, somebody will most definitely pull your card... and it's a lotta bottom feeders...but you ain't hear that from me." Carlotta grabbed a couple trays of food and handed one to Vicky as she followed her to a nearby table in the Day Room.

"I just hope and pray you don't gotta stay in here too long, seeing as how bubbly and vivacious you are. The world truly is a beautiful place to you, I can tell. Which is the last label you want to stick in this joint. That's when trouble really finds you. So I was just tryna help you out seeing as though I already *know* the game."

"Wow, so it was *you* who stepped in? Oh my gosh I owe you big time, I never even seen it coming."

"Yeah, I gathered that much. It was pretty obvious from the jump, but it's all good though - hey one for the team, right? I can already tell you're a good girl, though. It's written all over you. You probably think you gotta do something in order for people to dislike you or have beef but truth is, that ain't necessarily true. In this world, you don't have to do a single thing some folks not to like you. That's just how life is, in general. Besides, it was just way too painful to sit up here and witness you get your head peeled like that and not step in. Darn near had *me* in tears, Seriously. So you know nothing about that right or left hook jab... or you never heard of it... or what?"

"Hmmm... sounds relatively familiar."

"How about the *First Law of Defense*, is that ringing any sort of bell?"

"Absolutely nothing."

"I'm very sorry to hear that."

"No need to apologize, you can probably tell by now I'm pretty much not the fighting type."

"I concluded that much from the outcome, but just for future references or next time you find yourself in a possible scuffle, Self Preservation is *still* the First Law of Nature. You must always remember that."

"I guess I've just never really been the fighting type."

"I do understand... which is primarily why I was trying to allow you to keep that on the low... it also wouldn't hurt to sign up for a few Jujitsu classes in the meantime... Hey, just a suggestion. Another little tiny piece of friendly advice...next time you notice somebody bouta swoop in on you?"

"Uh huh." Vicky watched cluelessly as Carlotta balled up her fist and leaned back, then swiped the air. "Yeah, go ahead and try that one... just in case this is a re-occuring event. Definitely not an advocate of violence but like I mentioned earlier, self preservation is always the First Law of Defense... at your disposal."

"I'm probably not nearly as naive as I come off, though."

"I wholeheartedly would like nothing more than to believe that. Seriously." Carlotta snickered under her breath.

"You, on the other hand, definitely seem to know your stuff, however."

"Yeah, I been around the block a time or two. Been in a few female boxing competitions here and there. Loser to *none*, of course. Might even got a couple trophies here and there, who really knows."

"Awesome, that is truly impressive."

"*Awesome*? Where exactly are you from? Seriously, inquiring minds really wanna know."

"I grew up in Valley View."

"Who?"

"Valley...View."

"So like a *suburb* of a suburb."

"Basically."

"*Gotcha*...That explains it..."

"This is so unreal..." Vicky fought to keep her eyes open as the pain in the back of her head pounded all the way around to her temples, threatening to blind her as she fell across the table.

"That's it we're goin' back to the nurse, let's get it." Carlotta dropped her fork and slid back from the table.

"What happened to my painkillers?" Vicky fumbled through her purse as her head swirled with the room around her, growing lighter and lighter as she tried to pull forward, quickly slamming back onto the table face down. "I just came back from there, that's who gave me the prescription for my head."

"And we bouta head right back - let's go."

"I remember putting them right here in my purse." She pulled out a clump of loose tissue and a miniature bottle of hand lotion.

"Please tell me you didn't leave your purse on the table when you got in line..." Carlotta folded her arms in disbelief.

"Why not, I didn't go nowhere but to the lunch counter."

"Come on man, that's like a trip to Mars with these clowns, do you know how quick these shysters is up in here?"

"This is all happening so fast..." Vicky fought back the tears and massaged her temples as a shock of pain slammed into the back of her neck and rippled down her spine.

"And the earth is rotating a thousand miles an hour on its axis so pay attention, that's why your painkillers dissolved."

"Dissolved???"

"Yes...Diffused - ever heard of it?"

"I think so..."

"Yeah, we gotta get you up outta here soon as possible, Boo. Before they pick up on the gullibility factor... it'll be like blood to a shark."

"I'm *ready* to go."

"And I just bet you are, dear heart." Carlotta glanced across the room at Anita then reached out and helped Vicky up. "She's probably the one who clipped you."

"But how when we were fighting?"

"Correction... *she* was fighting... *you* were getting thrashed. Always know the difference. Regardless, either she did it while you was passed out or one of her cronies pick-pocketed you. Plain and simple."

"But wasn't no money in there, why would somebody steal some painkillers?"

"It's not always about money though, it could be one of two reasons in this case... finders keepers, possible consumption or make a profit.

Or both. Sorry that's three reasons, my bad."

"I had no idea painkillers were that highly sought after."

"Please, some people would injest just about anything to float away from the pain in their life, including Nitrous Oxide, if it was legal." Carlotta headed toward the doorway and whipped through the evil stares as they made their way toward the exit. "Yall's lookin mighty hard, you lost something or what? Cause I can *most definitely* help you find it." She quipped. "Ya might got the wrong one cuz I ain't never scared...remember that." She rolled her eyes at an entire room of instigators then nodded at Vicky and headed toward the door. "Let's go."

"I had no idea." Vicky followed, steadying herself as she braced against the hard concrete wall for support.

"Yeah...you good though. Like I said, stick with me I'll put you up on some hustle. Hopefully, it won't be too long before I get back on my feet."

"You seem pretty smart, how'd someone like *you* end up in a place like this?"

"I used to be a branch manager over a major financial institution before it went belly up and all hell broke loose. The whole thing crashed and so did I and everything I had went out the window. That's when I knew I had to scram. *Skidaddle*. In a honorable fashion, without rattin' nobody out. But I ain't speakin' on much. Long story short, I lost my job, we lost our home and *he stopped comin home*...and that's it in a nutshell."

"Who is he?"

"The hubby. I ended up divorced, homeless and on the streets all in one fell swoop. The rest is history."

"Bummer." Vicky made her way to the nurse's station for some replacement pain medication.

"Pretty much. From sugar to shinolah, as they say."

"He didn't even try to help you at all?"

"He who?"

"Your husband. Well I mean, your *ex*-husband."

"Nahhh, he's a coward. And that's with a capital 'C'."

"Any kids?"

"Thank goodness no, probably would've taken me out to see them going through this. What about you, what's your story?"

"Me? I been on my own since the age of twelve. Pops ran off when I was a baby and left mama all alone to fend for herself and ten kids. That's when everything went left and she end up all strung out on that stuff. The old man was a jerk for sure."

"Which is way nicer than I probably woulda put it, but you do you."

"Yeah, my great aunt did all she could to raise us but when she fell ill the old man couldn't keep his hands to himself and when she eventually passed I did the only thing I knew to do. And the streets been my home ever since."

"Wow, twelve years old having to survive the streets, I can't even imagine." Carlotta took a deep drag from her cigarette and leaned back, engulfed in a cloud of smoke, then handed it to Vicky.

"No thanks."

"Hey, I'm about to hook you up, check me out." She made her way over to another resident and struck up a conversation.

"She said you got some squares?" The heavy set woman limped in Vicky's direction and held out her hand.

"I don't even smoke." She shot Carlotta a puzzled look then glanced back at the weary looking woman dressed in rags.

"*Whatever*." The angry woman lurched away as Carlotta headed back to the table.

"But I just told you that I don't smoke, why would you even send her my way?"

"You don't, but I do...." She winked then reached into her pocket and pulled out a wad of singles and a few ten dollar bills. "That's what you call a *bona fide* goofy. A real buffoon, as we say from around the way." She snickered. "Sleeping Beauty didn't know whether she had Tens, Twenties or Fifties."

"So basically, you tricked her and then sent her over here so you could rip her off???"

"And your point is?" Carlotta stuffed the money back into her jacket pocket.

"But that's not right."

"And what that got to do with me?"

"I'm just saying, that's not fair."

"Neither is life."

"But that was just plain wrong."

"And how is this my fault?"

"I just believe you should do unto others as you would have them do unto you."

"Who told you that?"

"I was just raised brought up this way."

"Well I wasn't. I came up like you get yours and I'ma most definitely get mine. Plus, I don't like her."

"Why, what happened?"

"Nothing."

"So she did nothing for you to dislike her, I mean you don't even know her?"

"Don't have to. I just don't like her... simple as that. It's dog eat dog. You'll figure it out once you get tired of playin' the role of a simp..."

"Why does having a conscious make me a simpleton?"

"Dunno. You gotta ask *yourself* that one.. All I know is in *this* world, anything got to do with playin' it straight makes you not only a sucker, but gullible to any game any and everybody throws your way...at any given moment. Slim pickins for the culprits. Gotta run - peace out." Carlotta dashed off with no shame and disappeared down the long corridor then eased into the back hallway. "Easy prey." She whispered to Anita.

"I know. I'm still trying to figure out where she came from. With that level of wide-eyed innocence it's amazing she survived this long."

"Maybe you can offer her a crash course in *Reality*."

"Are you serious? ... I'm having way too much fun to stop now."

"You know any other time I'd be down for it - but she's so naive it's like taking candy from a baby." Carlotta stopped to think for a moment, considering the side effects her cruel actions may cause Vicky in the long run. "I just don't know... it's like kicking somebody when they're down."

"What better time to kick 'em?" Anita grimmaced. A sinister grin settling on the upward curves of her mouth as she snickered. "I mean, how you feel about yourself is how people treat you right?"

"Exactly... but how cruel is that?"

"Hey, it's a cruel old world we live in, what can I say. That's why you gotta kick them before they get a chance to kick you - wouldn't you agree? Afterall, if you give her a chance to get back up on her feet - you may never get the opportunity to kick her again... and how sad is that?" She sniffled. "Remember, opportunity only strikes once. Gotta keep that foot on her neck. Bite the snake before the snake bites you."

"What a way with words, you have."

"Thanks, 'preciate cha."

"You *would* say that."

"And you *should* say that - especially after what you just encountered. I mean, what's it gonna take for you to wake up... Seriously though... Call me what you like, but a person like you will always get tested ten times more than someone like me because that's just how the game goes. This world ain't tryna hear all that sentimental garbage and rhetoric. This world will run through you and right on over you. Eat you up and spit you out. It's every man, woman and dog for theyself. Where *you* been, under a rock?"

*****

Vicky made her way around the shelter as she surveyed the suspiciously empty halls, knocking from door to door. Never had it been this quiet, someone had to know something. Her mind flashed back to her ransacked room and missing items as she fished through her empty denim pockets searching for change as a trail of tears streamed down her face. *Nothing.* Anita had snuck in and stolen everything that wasn't nailed down. It would be another two days without anything to eat, she winced as a sharp pain pinched her in the right side just below her rib cage.

They were all in it together... Almost like a conspiracy. She thought to herself as she rushed toward the cafeteria which had been suddenly closing early for the last five days. All the vending machines were locked and no money to even buy a meal from the local dive across the street. She peered through the lunchroom window, wiping the tears away with the back of her sleeve as she searched for the lunch lady who had been evading her for days, in hopes of getting her name added to the boxed-dinner list.

Nervously pacing the halls she surveyed her options, overcome by desperation seeping in deeper and deeper, struck by the realization there was no one to call on. Even Carlotta had managed to stay out of sight. She turned toward her room and waved at the thin hooded figure. "Can you please help me?" It zig-zagged then dashed in the opposite direction as she entered her room and set on the edge of the cot examining the mess. Everything she owned, all of her belongings ransacked in a heap of clutter and alone again... She contemplated what had become of her life, questioning herself if it was really worth it.

From day one, everything had been a never ending struggle no matter how hard she tried to escape the madness...it always caught up...

Vicky examined all of the random items strewn across the room in a scattered pile of debris. It was all she had... and now even that was gone. She pulled herself up from the cot and entered the back hallway then headed down the stairwell, narrowly escaping a group of junkies as they huddled in a small cluster comparing paraphernalia, sizing her up as she dashed out the door.

The cool afternoon breeze of Fall stilled the gitters, washing away the stench of stale urine that pierced the shelter halls as she collected her thoughts, then crossed the street and headed toward the local diner and entered. "I was just wondering if yall had any leftover scraps...I ain't fussy just hungry..." She glanced around the diner filled with lunchtime patrons then back at the manager.

"Thought I told you don't come back round here again, woman." The stonefaced man dashed from behind the counter clenching his fists.

"Please, sir...I don't want no trouble, I'm just a 'lil bit hungry, that's all. Haven't eaten in days now somebody stole what little money I had left and went through all my things - I ain't got nothin' to my name. I'm stayin at the shelter 'cross the street and they keep skippin' over me with the meal boxes. They not doin' me right, please." She begged in exasperation.

"And it could potentially get a whole lot worse - you don't get outta my diner. My customers ain't tryna hear all your sob stories. Keep tryin my patience and you might get whatcha lookin for - I don't wanna lose my temper cause I just might not get it back."

"*But I really need help....*"

"Then I suggest you get on back over there where you came from and work it out 'cause I promise you - this ain't what you want. And you got five seconds to be on your merry little way or I'm callin' them Peoples on you and I mean it!" He shook his fist in the air then raced forward and shoved her out the door as she fell to the ground and crawled over to the garbage barrel. Then pulled herself up and walked a few blocks toward the medium framed church and went around to the back.

"Hello?" She grabbed the sturdy handle of the oak-trimmed door and peeked inside, then headed toward the basement for the food and donation line.

Chapter 2

"I want no parts of your wicked schemes." Vicky protested as she sat at a lunch table in the day room.

"Perfect, remain stuck if you want to, that's totally your prerogative... but if you knew like I know and how to hustle you wouldn't even be in a place like this. A place you aren't even equipped to comprehend - always having to watch your back. You don't belong here." Carlotta retorted sarcastically.

"And what about you?"

"Oh, I know how to survive."

"First you up and disappear on me - then show back up out of nowhere with a Ponzi-scheme?" Vicky countered defensively.

"You might look at it that way."

"Thanks, but I'm good."

"That all depends on who you ask."

"My point exactly, I'm not asking anyone for *anything*. I just want to get out of here the right way and put my life back together. Not land in even more hot water than I'm already in."

"That's why I'm trying to put you up on a little game. And I already told you I had to settle a little business right quick. But I'm back now, so just give it a try. You might surprise yourself and come up a winner for a change. Never know, it may be a whole new world out their waitin' on ya."

"I don't trust new worlds. What's in it for me, anyways?"

"So glad you asked." She pulled out a stack of envelopes. "Distribute these and in a day or two I'll have your money."

"What's in them?"

"Let's just say loan money."

"Like a loan officer?"

"Let's just say I offer people options who can't qualify for a conventional loan."

"But how does it make you money?"

"Interest."

"I don't know."

"Look, you wanna get paid right?"

"Depends...All money ain't good money."

"When you're stuck in a position like this it is because nobody is coming to bail you out, unless I missed something." She flipped the long fuchsia locks over her shoulder then unzipped her fanny pack and pulled out a wad of cash.

"How'd you get that?"

"Washing dishes, street vending... when I make money it allows me to lend it out and recoup a lender's fee."

"Does look quite appealing considering only thing I had to eat since the last couple of days was a bowl of soup. And that was *only* because the church up the street had mercy on my soul. Other than that, my ribs would be touching my back by now. And the lunch lady in here is pretty shady, she seems to go out of her way to make sure I *don't* get served. Dunno what she's got against me." Vicky watched as Carlotta rolled the ball between several cups daring for someone to make the winning selection.

"This is *My House*." She collected Five Dollars from each loser, snickering among the group of women as a crowd gathered to watch the ball shuffle beneath the cups for a second round. "Study long *Study Wrong*." Carlotta hyped the crowd in melodious banter.

"And No Cheating!" A random voice rang out from the crowd.

"You don't gotta cheat when you got the skills." Carlotta winked at the older man who suddenly appeared out of nowhere.

"Try *me* out." He pounded his chest then kneeled down in front.

"Sure about that?" She rearranged the cups with a smirk and reshuffled the ball.

"Hey, ya gotta pay the Cost if ya wanna be the Boss, right?" He quipped, pointing to a random cup as she lifted it up revealing the tiny ball.

"You got *lucky* that time." Carlotta picked up the objects and headed toward the lunch counter as the crowd dispersed to the sound of the dinner bell.

*****

"Thanks for standing up for me in there." Vicky leaned back on the cot in the dark as Carlotta lit a cigarette gazing out into the moonlit sky.

"Seems like everytime I make it to the lunch counter the cafeteria lady makes a point to close it down."

"Yeah, I remember. No worries, but you really do need to learn how to stand up for yourself, though. Can't just keep letting people walk all over you or you'll end up a doormat and never earn the respect you deserve." She inhaled and blew out a puff of smoke, then leaned over and picked up the tiny silver flask and took a sip of wine. "There's a reason she plays you like that, you know."

"Which is?"

"It's because she knows she can get away with it. You would *never* eat if it was up to her."

"But I did absolutely nothing to that woman."

"And you don't have to. Like I told you, in this life it takes nothing for someone to try or even despise you. People know who to test and who not to. Trust me."

"You think?"

"I *know*." Carlotta crushed the cigarette butt into the ashtray. "People will play you like a stooge for as long as you allow them to. It's truly baffling that you made it this far on your own."

"I just try to stay out the way."

"Good idea, but what about those who get in *your* way? That's the undeniable elephant in the room."

"I guess I just have to jump that bridge when I get to it."

"Well, if back there was any indication of your ability to jump the bridge - I say you most definitely fell in the water that time. All you need is a little more valiance though... and you're on your way. I promise you."

"Valiance?"

"Fortitude. You know, determination, street wisdom.... that *Know-How*."

"Know how to what?"

"Okay this might be alot more challenging than I bargained for, but you don't give up on me and I most definitely won't give up on you - how's that?"

"Deal."

"I see you got yourself an admirer." Carlotta peeped the older gentleman across the room as he made his way to the lunch counter.

"He speaks from time to time, once in a while we chit chat."

"He looks more interested than just chatting, if you ask me... Pops ain't too hard on the eyes neither. You can look at his clothes and tell he might have a few coins stashed away somewhere. Definitely an Old School Playa right there. You better watch out. That's that *Goldman Sachs* swag. Cashmere slacks. Foldies... All he needs is some "Temptations" music playing in the background. The real question is how did *he* end up in this joint." Carlotta sized him up from head to toe.

"I think he might work here...not quite sure what he does, though."

"And that's exactly what you're about find out."

"I am?"

"Why sure you are."

"But why me???"

"Why not you? And don't go to gettin' all shy on me now - I checked him checking you out, so it's the perfect match."

"Really? I hadn't noticed."

"Well I did. You should give Mac Daddy a little conversation... Ya know, feel him out...find out what he's made of... *And even what he ain't.*"

"I'm straight."

"Hey, don't sleep on it. I'd hate to see you miss out... Never know, that could be the love of your life."

"I wouldn't go that far."

"Seriously though, how many stories have you heard from people who met some long lost love and then they get all starry eyed, looking off into the distance and what not, reminiscing in detail about the forlorn days of yesteryear and the long lost love of their life?"

"Never?"

"Then you haven't lived. Besides, when was the last time someone took you out on a romantic date?"

"Been a while."

"*C'mon* waddaya got to lose." Carlotta patted her on the shoulder and parted ways.

*****

"Greetings." She approached the hazel complexioned silver fox as he poured some tobacco onto a thin slip of paper and licked the edges, then rolled it into a homemade cigarette.

"My My My... Heaven gotta be missin' an angel, I'm Ralph and you are?" His eyes filled with subtle mischief as he looked up from his minor project.

"Vicky." She smiled innocently.

"I don't believe we've met - if so, sentence me now cuz I had to have been fresh outta my mind to have *ever* overlooked such a magnificent wild-flower like you queen. And that's on *everythang* I love."

"What can I say, I'm speechless." She soaked in his handsome appearance and chuckled, captivated by his easy-going charm and wit.

"And I'm *honored*...If I could be so obliged or you would be so kind as to tell me - what is your full name...*beloved*."

"Victoria, but everybody just calls me Vicky."

"Ahhhh... Vicky...that ain't too tricky. So what brings you to the Salvation of Army Estates?"

"Just down on my luck I guess."

"Don't sound too copacetic to me, why is that?"

"Life."

"Sorry to hear it - sure wish there was something I could do."

"Honestly, any little bit could help." She gazed into his eyes for a moment then quickly shifted her attention as she studied the floor.

"Like?"

"You tell me."

"I see you like to cut straight to the chase. No riff-raff."

"None at all. Like I said, I'm grateful for whatever. But I don't wanna stress you though - or whatever it is you got goin'."

"You good... Let me see what I can do..." He rustled through his pockets and pulled out a few singles.

"Thanks." She fluttered her lashes. "I was just wondering if you knew how long that might take 'cause I need to get back to the nurse, I got jumped in here you know?"

"So sorry to hear that."

"Yeah, they got down on me."

"Who is *they*?"

"Some occupant in the lunch area."

"Word?"

"Yup."

"That's a low down shame, you way too beautiful to get jumped."

"Thanks, you're not so bad yourself. So you work out this way or just passing through?"

"I'm in what you call a transitional period. I got laid off my last gig but one of my partners 'bout to get me on at Universal Steel. They looking for part-time workers. Hey, it's better than nothing, so I'm most definitely not complainin' I'm just explainin', so to speak."

"What's the pay, maybe I can get on too."

"Queen, you don't look like the steel worker type, you really think you could handle it?"

"Like you said, something is better than nothing right?"

"Right-right. I guess they start off around ten dollars an hour comin' in the door. They probably can find you a lil' *light duty* - Keep ya nice and dainty. Let me see if I can pull some strings and I'll get right back at cha."

"That'll work and thank you so very much. So what you do there?"

"Me, I'm a certified welder for over Thirty years."

"Seniority, wow I'm impressed."

"Don't worry about it Queen, you In Like Flynn. Like I said, it's only a matter of time before I get back on again." He reached inside his pocket and pulled out a card then handed it to her. "Just gimme a call."

Chapter 3

It felt like forever, but the day had only just begun. Ralph pondered to himself as he sat on the curbside of the main boulevard processing his thoughts, the loud ruckus immediately commanding his attention as he quickly rose to his feet, anxiously scanning the area as the wild-eyed barefoot woman ran up on him in a cloud of fury.

"HE'S AFTER ME!!" She rushed toward Ralph screaming to the top of her lungs as she grabbed his jacket then stumbled to the ground and laid at his feet.

"*WHO???*" He jumped up to comfort her as he looked up and down the street.

"Get Back Here Woman!" The delusional man charged out of nowhere and pounced, lifting her up in the air as she tumbled helplessly back to the ground, pinned beneath his weight as Ralph dived to the rescue. Momentarily dazed by the madman's forceful blow as it met with the side of his jaw pounding like a ton of bricks, he staggered backwards then quickly rebounded, charging straight ahead in a tumultuous headbutt as he crashed into his gut dropping him to his knees.

"*Don't worry, I got you.*" Ralph helped the woman up and pulled her into his arms, rocking her back and forth as the street urchin scuffled to his feet and ran off..

"He's a crazy man!" She sobbed frantically into his chest.

"Who is he to you?" Ralph grabbed the woman's hand and led her across the street as they walked past the crowd of spectators to an old abandoned building and sat on the steps.

"He's my husband and I know he's coming back... *Please* protect me." She whimpered.

"He can try but I promise you this, I will personally rock his frame." Ralph looked her square in the eye.

"He's nuts, he won't leave me alone." She broke down in tears.

"That part's on him, trust me, I don't scare too easy. He'll learn a valuable lesson if he comes this way. I'm not an advocate for violence but I do believe we have to protect ourselves when the time comes and I'm definitely not about to just stand around and watch a man put his hands on a woman. That's a pretty cowardly act. Have you contacted law enforcement?"

"I've tried everything from restraining orders to protection orders, but he just keeps finding his way back to me and now I don't know what to do anymore." She trembled uncontrollably.

"You don't have anywhere to go, no family or friends?"

"Everybody wrote me off." She sobbed into her hands.

"Why?"

"Nobody cares about me, I guess."

"I care." He reached out and stroked her shoulder.

"Please don't leave me." She grabbed hold of his hand and held on tight. "I'm so scared he's gonna come back."

"Let's go." He led her to his car and helped her inside, then drove toward the Salvation Army Center.

"Where you takin' me?" She looked out the window from the back seat, rocking side to side from the effects of the pills.

"Hey, you gotta level with me... you sober or not?" Ralph pulled over on a side street.

"Every once in awhile I might take a drink." She looked away then back out the window.

"I been out here too long on these streets lady, sorry try again. Like I said, if you want me to help you I need honesty. You gotta be straight with me."

"I'll take the fifth." She slumped over and gazed down at the floor for a moment.

"I really hate to hear you say that. You're too beautiful of a young lady with your whole life ahead of you, why?" Ralph looked away in deep thought.

"Life is hard."

"Hey, everybody is goin' through something, but that's no excuse to let your whole life swirl down the drain. Do you have any idea just how many people lose their lives to controlled substances everyday?"

"Forgive me, I hadn't bothered to do the math." She rolled her eyes and looked away.

"Joke all you want but the numbers will blow your mind, hundreds of thousands every year. That's nothing to sneeze at - I'd be taking those statistics pretty seriously if I were you.... *Hello???*" He watched as she dozed off then snapped his fingers.

"I hear ya..." Vicky straightened up for a second and ran her fingers through her long platinum mane of twists then slumped forward again.

"Why would you even allow yourself to get hooked on that crap, you got way more sense than that I know."

"Thanks, try telling the old man that. Everytime he sees me he wants to reach out and touch me if you know what I mean. All he ever wants to do is fight."

"Why do you take it though, that's the million dollar question right there."

"Don't have nowhere to go, so what's the point? Wherever I try to hide it's only a matter of time before here he comes... and the thrashing is always worse than the last. So I just learned to stay put." Her voice slurred as she drifted in and out.

"How long you been together?"

"Fifteen years..." She leaned over in the seat and laid down.

"Was he always this brutal, I mean what happened - what set him off?"

"It wasn't always like this, he used to be really good to me. Then like all of a sudden out of nowhere, one day he just switched up on me. Next thing I know, that was it."

"Just outta the blue?"

"Exactly."

"Wow that's gotta suck..."

"Truly it does."

"Maybe it was always there and you just didn't notice it. Probably hid it really well." Ralph glanced up in the rearview mirror.

"Probly, but it like came outta nowhere and all a sudden everything just seemed like it pissed him off."

"Like?"

"Say for instance, if he saw another man checking me out - I got it. Even if I didn't even know the person, all bets were off... Or if he asked me to bring him something and I seemed to be moving too slow for his taste - it was on again."

"*Geezzz* Louise... I'm so sorry to hear you been through all this. It's a wonder you're still around to even talk about it..." Ralph pulled over to collect his thoughts. "This is a serious matter."

"I stay prayed up, that's all I can do."

"And that's your best bet. I wanna ask you a quick question, if you don't mind."

"Go for it."

"Is *he* sober?"

"No comment...."

"C'mon, you gotta get off that stuff, it's obviously not helping either one of you in the situation. You know there's help for you if you want it, but can't nobody do the work *for you*. You gotta *want it*. It's all up to you, but you gotta want to get better. Have a better existence... live a better life..."

"I do want better, but this crap just won't leave me alone. I try and I try... but it's like I get so sick and I can't pull it together even if I wanted to. It's like I can't even function on my own." Vicky sat up for a moment then fell back down as her eyes rolled to the back of her head.

"Hey, you okay?" Ralph hopped out the car and ran around to the back passenger door and quickly dialed 911.

*****

The evening sky echoed with sadness as Ralph made his way back to his car and sat in deep thought. It felt like the entire world was going crazy and nobody seemed to care. He tried to relax as he let back his seat trying to figure it all out as his heart pounded against his chest, then started the car and headed back to the boulevard.

The streets were unusually quiet as he combed the area. The evening crowd was finally tapering down as the familiar gaunt figure dashed across the street capturing his attention. He had to get to the bottom of it as quickly as possible, he switched lanes and followed the haggard vagrant down the street, then pulled over and hopped out the car on a wild foot chase around the block, hemming him up in a corner.

"Hey, back up off me man." An evil look crossed the attacker's face as his back met the wall.

"Look, you not phasing me bruh. Now you can keep going around intimidating women and damsels in distress if you wanna, but a real man ain't afraid to square up with you. Pal." Ralph clenched his fingers around his collar and pulled in face to face.

"I'm tellin' you, this here ain't what you want." The crazed man whispered in rage.

"Why not try me and find out." Ralph whispered back unbothered, his rockbound reserve placid as the evening sky.

"Look man, I don't want no trouble. I'm just minding my own business hoping you do the same, aight? This is between me and my old lady. Who you supposed to be - the Feds???"

"I'm whoever you need me to be, buddy. I can just see you're headed down the wrong path so I'm here to straighten you out. Especially if you think I'm about to sit up here and watch you take advantage of a woman or anybody else who can't defend themselves - and expect me not to step in and do something about it. You sincerely got me twisted, my man." Ralph squared up again.

"I don't take too kindly to threats, Sir." He snatched away.

"Well, we got something in common then cause I don't take too kindly to bullies, either. It's about a certain code of ethics... Honor. My job is to protect women, children and the vulnerable of society and that's just what I'm gonna do. I run the Young Adult At Risk Program, regardless of whether or not it's teens, juveniles or grown folks - best believe I'm doin' what I can to help *But I'm Getting Tired Of This Man!*" Ralph snatched him up again by his collar.

"Hey, no need to raise your voice, it don't take all that to get your point across. You don't even have a clue what I, myself, been through." He faced Ralph man to man.

"Look, we all have been through our share of pain, but that does not give you an excuse to go around mistreating and taking advantage of others. I get so tired of people like you taking out your anger on people who can't fight back or stand up for themselves. Come on man, *Man Up!*"

"I DID MAN UP!!! I had to fight my old man everyday to protect my mama. Do you know what it's like to watch your pops take your mother's life!!! Do you have any idea?!?!?" He snatched away and slammed into the wall then slid down to the ground. "I watched that rogue take her whole life... when all she ever did was try to love that creep. She did all she could for our family and he *still* took her away from us... he took my soul, man." He whimpered like a baby. "Do you know what it's like to have to bury your mama at the age of fifteen?? I was just a kid, dude... She was all I had!!!"

"I hear you man, I hear you." Ralph sat down beside the young man and squeezed him tight. "That's crazy."

"Every blow to this world is like a swing on the old man, in restitution for what he did to my mama. I couldn't even cry at his funeral. I detested that clown."

"I understand and I'm sorry that happened, but this ain't the way man. As painful as it is... this ain't the way. And she is not your father. You just can't go through life taking out your anger on other people because you're hurt, because you've been wronged. It still won't bring her back. It's only gonna make things worse...for you and everybody who comes in contact with you. But it's gonna continue to live on in *your* own heart, like poison. And eventually you will be the one to succumb to it. You will be the one to pay the ultimate price because that type of rage will take you right out of here. Trust me.

And it's only a matter of time before it lands you in trouble or you break down an innocent person who doesn't deserve it. That queen did nothing to deserve what you did to her." Ralph's stern words reverberated into the atmosphere.

"I'm just tired man... I'm tired of life... I'm tired of living."

"Hey, you gotta get tired enough to change, though. That's the key. And I'm not saying it's gonna be easy, neither. But it will be *worth* it in the end."

"I know, but where do I start? Ain't nobody trying to hire a bum like me. Nobody's trying to give me a chance. People don't even want me around. They don't care if I live or die. Here I am twenty-four years old and I feel like a Hundred and Ten. Like I got nothin' to live for."

"That's just not true. But I will say this... it's only a matter of time before you meet your match or *your Maker*. And either way you gonna have to pay the piper. Pay for what you've done in this life. So you may as well straighten up and fly right. What do you have to lose? At least that's the way I see it." Ralph stood to his feet and paused for a moment.

"True." The tall gaunt man quivered as he concentrated for a second, then slowly eased up off the ground. "But where do I start?"

"Glad you asked." Ralph led him to his car and headed over to the drug rehab center. "By the way, what's your name son?"

"Bryant..." The young man stared at the tall brick building with iron clad bars on the window. "Hey, they gone lock me up in there or what?"

"I'm Ralph... and to answer your question. No... this is just a facility where you can get clean, get back up on your feet and get on a clear path to employment. Let's just say it's an opportunity to get the help you need while they monitor and assist you in getting off the streets, all in one rip. And you can't beat that cause it ain't nothing out here in these streets but trouble and it's only a matter of time before you find it or it finds you... again and again and again.

"All you gotta do is follow the rules, regulations and guidelines. And most of all, stay out of trouble. And in return they're going to help wean you off of all that mess you got up in your system, help you through that nasty withdrawl and get you legally and gainfully employed. Anybody who wouldn't take advantage of this opportunity needs to have their head examined... Let's face it, a lot of people *wish* they had it. It's not everyday you get a second chance to get it right - so don't mess it up 'cause it only takes one slip and you'll be right back to square one before you know it... Got it?"

"Word." The ragged young man climbed out the car and followed Ralph into the building.

*****

"So what's the low-down?" Carlotta lit the tip of her cigarette and leaned forward. "I need details for *inspiration*."

"I take it you mean information." Vicky studied her face for a reaction.

"See what I mean? I know you better than you know yourself. Now all I need for you to do is trust the process - you got more potential than you'll ever know. But never fear, Big Sis is here to guide the way to help you develop into your full potential."

"Thanks, now I can finally sleep at night. Anyway, he seems to be a stand-up guy from what I can tell."

"And what is *your* definition of stand-up?"

"You know, hardworking... committed. He got laid off at the steel mill so he's just filling in doing some custodian work for the time being.

He seems like a nice guy. Who knows, he may even be able to get me on down there on a little light duty detail."

"How snazzy." Carlotta blew out a puff of smoke. "Please, no time for the mushy stuff let's just get right down to the skinny. Is he or ain't he loaded?"

"What do you want from me, I can't just go up and start quizzing this guy about his finances."

"And why not?"

"I'm just not built that way."

"Sorry to hear that. On a different note, I knew it was something about him from the jump, he just doesn't blend in here. I mean he do, but then again he *don't*. He's definitely no ordinary Joe Schmoe, that's for sure."

"How can you tell?"

"Look at his hair for starters, all faded up and trimmed to the tee. Plus, that five-o-clock shadow he's working with ain't no joke. Pops is in there, trust me on this one."

"Well, he said he's in transition from a brief lay off until he gets back on his feet."

"And we're about to transition right along with him."

"We are?"

"Absolutely."

"To where, though?"

"That's what we need you to find out."

"Me again?"

"Congratulations, you're a popular choice." Carlotta saluted.

"Gee, and I never even auditioned."

"No worries, you just got signed up, Boo."

"Where can I get unsigned?"

"I'll keep you posted. Besides, never sleep on your talent, you're perfect for the role. A real *au la naturel*...you just need someone to help you to bring it out. Help you set better goals for your life. You know, bring out the winner in ya, so to speak."

"Thanks. I *think*."

"No worries... Did you happen to mention to him that all your stuff is stuck in a storage unit, which is about to be thrown out on the streets if you can't come up with the cash, but you don't have it because you just don't got it like that?"

"Wow, I wasn't even aware that was going on in my own life."

"Hey learn something new every day, you know?"

"I've just never been the type to take advantage of people."

"Which is just what makes you the natural sweetie you are, he'll never hear the thunder." Carlotta winked.

"How is that?"

"Well on the one hand, your naivety pays off big time because it definitely plays in your favor. And your innocence and goofiness just tops it all off. Which is also why you get played in life the way that you do. But on the other hand, it can cause you to appear so unsuspecting that some people underestimate your intelligence and let down their guards - which can ultimately end up giving you the upperhand. Therefore, being the scapegoat is not always such a bad thing, afterall. You just gotta know how to play it. It's the pre-requisites of Survival of

The Fittest Course 101."

"Where can I download that App?" Vicky reassessed her point of view.

"In life there are no downloadable Apps, shortcuts or guarantees. You either got it or you don't. And if you don't, you just gotta learn the hard way. This is a crazy world we live in, you can go your whole life being the nice guy. Trying to do everything right, like a Goodie Two Shoes and guess what? You still run the risk of getting played because the world is a battlefield. It's just a fact of life. This world can be very deceiving, so you may as well come in and go out swinging. Just a word to the wise...Right, wrong or indifferent. It just is what it is." Carlotta winked mischievously.

"Thanks for the free psycho-analysis."

"Just calling it like I see it. Let's look at it like a leisure recreational.... hobby."

"I don't know, everything's just moving so fast."

"And the earth is rotating on its axis even faster, your point is? Come on, you can't keep coming up with all these reasons."

"Reasons for what?"

"Excuses will get you nowhere. In this world there's always going to be someone out there who can see you doing good and still try to do everything in their power to block you. But when the shoe is on the other foot and you do wrong? You gotta pay your dues... unless you're smart. In this world the good guys always finish last. Remember that. So you just gotta always stay prepared... up on your game, so to speak. Either way you better know how to move. Or *get* to know... Just a little encouragement, if you will."

"I'll admit I'm not perfect, but I do try to do what's right. At least seventy percent of the time."

"Those are the ones who catch it the most are you kidding me? Take yourself for example... you probably tried to be a good person your whole entire life and look what happened. Life got in the way, you ended up in a situation you had absolutely no control over and on your own at twelve years of age. See how that works? Did you ask for that to happen to yourself? No you didn't. Is it fair? No it isn't. It just is what it is. Let's be honest, prim and proper will never pay the bills. Good people get exploited for their goodness every day of the week."

"So people don't want to see me come up, is basically what you're saying."

"Put it this way, the world is not boiling over with unrequited love. There may be a few people who are genuinely happy for you, but I wouldn't bet on it if I were you. Misery loves itself some company. It's okay to be a little naive when you're a kid, but come on man, let's not remain a sucker. At least not our entire life. There's just no excuse. Everybody wants to believe there's enough to go around, and in a sense, there may even be an inkling of truth in that. But in a even *greater truth,* that's probably one of the greatest lies that's ever been told because everyone isn't to be trusted. Trust and *believe.* So it's all up to you. You can choose to stand strong or fall for every gimmick that comes your way, choice is yours. Know your role in life, as well as the roles of others. What role they play in your life and or what role they're coming to play. Stay on your toes. And remember, the side you were born on ain't always the side you wanna *be* on."

"That's golden wisdom."

"Hey, you might not be able to control that next man, but you can catch that frog before it leaps... All day long. I prefer to know what I'm dealing with off the cuff. But let's just explore how we can help your boy help us. You said he has connections right?"

"He just said he might be able to put in a good word for me."

"Connections."

"I guess helping to line me up for work opportunities and maybe a place to stay equals connections..."

"I think you owe him a big ole sloppy hug, don't you?" Carlotta grimaced.

"I'm still processing..."

"Just how generous of a fellow is he?"

"On an apartment?"

"On anything."

"Don't know."

"Well I think it's a fine time you find out, don't you?"

*****

"Five Hundred." Vicky sat at the corner table in the day room across from Ralph.

"Five *Who???*" He picked up a Q-tip to clean out his ears.

"I need Five Hundred Dollars."

"Just like that?"

"You did say you could help me, right?"

"All depends on your definition of help."

"Compassion not charity."

"Whatever you need it to be, I guess."

"Help to get back on the right track... in life."

"Five Hundred Dollars would set a whole lots of folks back on the right track. Question is, what track are you trying to get on?"

"A decent coat...clothes... Just in case a job opportunity comes up I need to be able to represent myself. That way even if you do lean on somebody to get me into an apartment I can at least contribute something to the cause." Vicky fluttered her long lashes.

"You sure are a beautiful lil' thang, ya know that right?" His eyes combed her shapely physique.

"Why thank you, kindly." She smiled demurely.

"Let me see what I can do... In the mean and in between, when was the last time you had something to put on your stomach?"

"I did have a little something for breakfast but I will take a fruit tray, that is if you don't mind..."

"*One fruit box comin' right up.*" He flung his leather jacket across the back of his chair then pulled out a stack of bills.

"Thanks so much." Vicky watched quietly as he headed toward the lunch counter then quickly checked her surroundings to make sure the coast was clear as she slipped her hand inside the coat pocket and clutched a few bills, quickly stashing them into her blue jeans as he grabbed the styrofoam container and plastic fork.

"For the most beautifulest woman on the planet... on *my* planet, anyway." He made his way back to the table, beaming from ear to ear as he set down the plate.

"Looks yummy." Vicky opened the box and gazed over the luscious assortment of fruit. "Oops, did I forgot to mention I'm allergic to pickles?"

"No problemo, fresh and clean for my queen - ." He quickly swept up the box and zipped back toward the counter.

"Thanks Zaddy you're the best." She smiled as she watched him conversate with the lunch attendant, then eased her hand back into his jacket pocket and clipped a few more bills.

*****

"So how much you get from that clown?" Carlotta watched as Vicky pulled out the crumpled up bills and tossed them onto the cot.

"Not bad for a rookie." She surveyed the bucks, picking them up one by one and straightening them out. "I gotta get outta dodge, though."

"Why is that?" Vicky sat on the floor indian style and folded her legs.

"They after me."

"And who is *they*?" She continued to quiz.

"Nobody." Carlotta held up her fist in solidarity then headed for the door. "Stay down, I'll get back."

Chapter 4

Tension loomed in the sky like a dark cloud as Ralph made his way around the old neighborhood running his usual deliveries for the Young Adult program, when the broken image of a frail weary figure crouched in the doorway of the corner store caught his eye.

"Will you let me help you?" He knelt down next to the tiny figure and whispered in her ear.

"I want revenge." The fragile woman peeked beneath the worn hood of the oversized trench coat, shivering as she spat out the venomous words.

"What happened to you???" He pulled her close gently embracing her delicate frame.

"She stole my husband and everything I had." The feeble woman rocked back and forth as a trail of tears trickled down her face. "And I really thought she was my friend... *I trusted her.*" She weeped in agony.

"I am SO sorry." Ralph ran his fingers through her thick matted hair then gently lifted her chin as he looked into her sorrowful eyes, her head hung low as she sobbed in hearted-broken desperation.

"I will never forgive either one of them. Her or him. I wish they both would just go away. She took everything I had from me. My heart, my joy, the love of my life *and my life*."

Ralph listened intensively as she poured out her heart then spoke, carefully measuring his words. "But there is one thing they could *never* take from you - no matter how hard they or anyone else tries. Or how deep the betrayal cuts or who casts the stone - they still miss." He consoled her.

"What're you talking about? I had a complete nervous breakdown and had to be hospitalized. Then on top of that, I ended up in a psych ward and I didn't even know I was crazy!!! I'll *never* forgive those two." She pounded her fist against the pavement.

"I know it hurts.... trust me, I *know*." He pulled her into his arms and held her tight.

"I tried everything in my power to forgive him and his woman, that *so-called best friend of mine*, but they did me dirty... I even prayed for them and tried to be friends with them despite how they crossed me out and they just laughed at me like I was a fool and rubbed it all in my face. And oh how they laughed, while I sat at home alone crying myself to sleep at night - asking myself over and over again why me? Questioning and wondering what I had ever done to deserve two of the very people I trusted with my whole life and loved so dearly, to forsake me like that. Two people I would have done anything for...

"Do you know how it feels for someone to laugh in your face after they've done you wrong and they know it - and there's not even a glimmer of remorse for the wrong they've committed??? It hurts me to my soul. It's like a pain I can never put into words... all I know is it never stops paining and I did not deserve this."

"Trust me, *I been there*. Maybe not in the exact same way, but I definitely been betrayed many many times throughout my life." Ralph confided with compassion.

"But I let this woman come into my home. I took this woman in and offered her food and shelter... a safe place to stay in the middle of her storm. I even let her borrow my clothes and this is how she repays me? Where's the justice? I mean, what part of the game is this, because if this is my part I want no parts of it!!"

"Wow...I'm speechless... I don't even know what to say. And I know it takes time for wounds like this to heal and it definitely ain't comin' over night." Ralph felt his heart sink into the pit of his stomach as he uttered the tender words of compassion in an attempt to ease her strife.

"Do you know I even went down to my job and asked them to consider her for an open position and then picked up an application for her to fill out only to come home and find her in bed with my husband? I fight for her to get gainfully employed and she climbs into bed with my husband?!?"

"Unspeakable." Ralph shook his head in disbelief. "What happened next?"

"You mean after I went ballistic?"

"Okay..."

"I threw her out of my house along with that creep of a husband of mine, that's what."

"But then you let him back in? I'm just asking..."

"We went to a marriage counselor and tried to work on it but I eventually just gave up. I just couldn't do it anymore. I tried everything I could to save our marriage, but I got tired of playing the fool."

"I do understand. And betrayal is very difficult to overcome. It's a bitter pill to swallow but we have to forgive in order to move on."

"I had to be medicated *and* regenerated. Seek counseling to keep from losing my grip, which I probably had already lost it but was too far gone to even realize. And just as I was starting to let my guard down again and I let him back in and we eventually got back together and vowed to work on our marriage - guess whose number I find in his phone?"

"Mannn...that's crazy." Ralph dropped his head in disbelief for a moment. "Then what happened?"

"Of course, he denied it. But that was it for me and I left his no good self for good that time. So they ended up getting back together because he had no place else to go and this here well had most definitely run dry. But they eventually just had to move right across the street from me and everyday I was forced to witness their public displays of affection, gallivanting and prancing around in front of me. Taunting me. Flaunting their love affair in my face. I was on the verge of giving up... ending it all. But I eventually got away."

"This is one of the most heart-wrenching stories that has ever crossed my path and I cannot even fathom what you must have possibly gone through." Ralph handed her a tissue and gently stroked her back.

"But that ain't all..."

"Please don't tell me there's more."

"Of course there's more - she actually got the friggin' job! Needless to say I quit the next day."

"*No way*."

"Hey, I can't make this stuff up Sir." The young woman leaned back to light her cigarette.

"Can I tell you something that you may not believe or want to hear?"

"At this point, what have I got to lose, how could it possibly get any worse - or need I ask?" The weary woman rolled her eyes in resignation and defeat.

"Sometimes when people are removed from your life – even though it can often be extremely hurtful and painful - believe it or not, *everything* happens for a reason. And in the end, it is probably the best thing that could have ever happened *to you and for you* because that person could have ended up causing so much more damage that may have even destroyed you. Trust me. And I know you're probably wondering or asking yourself, how much worse could the situation actually have gotten....I mean, you got a bestie who turned on you and turned out to be your worst enemy... and your worst nightmare, so to speak. Then you have a husband who you've taken vows with for better or worse, although not this worse I know, and devoted yourself to him as a faithful wife. Yet, he betrayed you in one of the most horrendous ways. Nevertheless, do take heed, because there is *still* an upside to all of this... Which is, that you got away from two very toxic spirits because when you are dealing with a spirit of betrayal, jealousy and deceit at this level - you never know just how deep it runs. And at the end of the day, there's just no telling how low a person with that much malice in their heart could have stooped. And that goes for either one of them."

"You know, I never even thought about it that way. Thank you for the enlightenment."

"See, you have to ask yourself the tough questions... look at it like this - what reason did he really have to betray you? Especially at this level. In your heart of hearts, only you know the true answer to that question. But from the way you explain things, it looks to me like you were good to him. A good wife for him. You even forgave him several times for his transgressions and repeatedly stepping out on you within the marriage when many would have not - even for the first time."

"Yes it took everything out of me." She leaned over and began sobbing again.

"I'm sure. And the same goes for her, not to even mention the abhorrence of it being with your best friend to add even more salt to the wound and insult to injury - not to mention, you thought she was your best friend so she had your trust and she abused it."

"But why???"

"I mean that's the million dollar question with people who drain you of all you got and it's still not enough... it's almost like they're trying to completely destroy you, which is indeed sinister. I mean, you looked out for this woman. Even got her a job - but she turned on you in the end... for seemingly no reason at all. Trust me, that kind of betrayal and that level of deceit does not go unnoticed. There will be retribution. It's just not in your hands. But there's a heavy price to pay, it's just not up to you to decide.

"But you seem like a very strong person with a good humble heart and I do believe there are great things in store for your future, however, you can't go on living your life this way. Beating yourself up and punishing yourself for what others have done to you. Now they win twice, because not only did they hurt and betray you the first time but now you are hurting and betraying yourself. You must find a way to accept it and forgive so that you can move on and allow yourself to heal....to be free... No matter how hard it may seem. Vengeance does not belong to us."

"But where do I possibly begin? I am broken in pieces...."

"Believe me, time and prayer heals all wounds even though some scars still remain, you should on the other hand, be exceedingly grateful that these things were revealed to you now. And that you no longer have to deal with these conspirators any longer. Be at peace, because according to their actions and character - it could have only gotten worse."

"So what are you saying?"

"That union was never meant to be..."

"But I feel so powerless."

"Because the *power* is not in your hands."

"I even lost my job... my spirit was so broken I was unable to work. Do you know how degrading that is after all those years of hard work, education and dedication I put into building my career? All of the trials and sacrifice and long-suffering I endured trying to hold on to my marriage for twenty wasted years of my life. And then to lose everything I had worked so hard for and end up on the streets like this??? I hate him!!!"

"Be careful...the tongue is a very powerful and unruly member. It can bring life and it can bring death. You shall have what you say, beloved." Ralph whispered as the tears rolled down his face, a heavy vibration banging in his chest from the rage and torment in her eyes and in her heart.... as he paused for a moment to collect his thoughts. "I need you to listen... and listen to me very carefully. All of these things may have broken your heart and taken all of your worldly possessions, but they could never break your spirit unless you allow them to. The soul of who you are and who God called you to be." He lifted her head again and looked into her downcast eyes. "You may be downtrodden, but you will heal from this. You will smile again and bounce back whole and seven times stronger than you ever were before. Iron sharpeneth iron."

"But they wrote me off and left me to wither away." She broke down in tears again.

"I understand all that, but you still have to find a way to forgive them or you will not be forgiven. And I'm not saying it's going to be easy. Nothing in this life worth accomplishing ever is, but it's the only way you can begin to heal."

"But it's just not fair, what happens to them and all of the pain they caused in my life, how can they get up and just walk away after all of the hurt and destruction they've caused?"

"You can't worry about them, you can only worry about you. Focus on getting your spirit right - the rest is on them. Each person bears the responsibility for their own actions. Trust me, it all comes back in the end, don't worry about it. Just get your business in order and make sure your heart and your spirit is right. Let's just focus on getting you straight and back up on your feet for now. Because without a clear head, you can't make clear decisions... any children by the way?"

"We were never able to conceive."

"Hmmm... I see. So where will you go from here?"

"Well, I can sign myself back into the psyche ward for another evaluation... but I don't want to do that..." She contemplated.

"Were they helping you?"

"Sorta..."

"Was there a long-term plan in place?" Ralph stood and reached out his hand then helped her to her feet.

"Well, if I stick with the program and work my way through it, they will help me get into a work program from there."

"Sounds like a definite plan. How old are you - if you don't mind me asking?"

"Forty years young."

"That's the spirit. Hey, it ain't never too late for a come back right?" He held out his fist for a fist pump.

"Right." She met him knuckle to knuckle then followed him to his car." I had almost graduated from the program but I relapsed and started using again. The pain got too deep and I couldn't cope." She climbed in the car as they rode toward the mental health center.

"You ready?" He parked in the lot and looked into the rearview mirror.

"I'm ready to change my life." She pulled the lapels of the oversized trench coat closed. "I'm tired. But I wanna do better. I *need* to do better.... I *deserve* better. I wanna be free."

"Hey, that's all you had to say, young lady. That's good news. That's where it all begins. And *exactly* what it's gone take. Just remember this, it's always darkest right before daybreak, Queen." He hugged her as they headed toward the building. "Just remember one thing...you got this, Sis."

*****

"I need to ask you a few questions." The case worker stood in the doorway for a moment, his eyes combing the tiny room of the shelter.

"What's this all about?" Vicky sat up on the edge of the cot nervously as the outside voices in the hallway fell to a low whisper.

"Mr. Miller, Department of Human Services." He entered the room then reached out to shake her hand. "And you are?"

"Vicky."

"Vicky.... and your last name?"

"Jones."

"Carlotta Smith. You know her?"

"Vaguely. She used to share this room with me but that's just about all I know."

"When's the last time you spoke with her?" He pulled out a pen and pad and began writing.

"I haven't."

"What do you mean you haven't, I thought you just said she shared a room with you." He folded his arms across his chest and leaned back.

"I said she *used* to. She left about a week ago and I haven't seen nor heard from her since."

"Just like that?"

"Yes."

"Did she say where she was going?"

"That's all I know." Vicky could feel the tension as he stared through her.

"So she was in a hurry..." He jotted some more information onto his pad.

"I didn't say that."

"So what *are* you saying?"

"All she told me was that she was leaving."

"What would cause her to just up and leave so suddenly, though?"

"I didn't say it was suddenly."

"You said she was your roommate right?"

"Correct."

"Okay, so one minute you're sharing a room with someone then out of the blue, next thing you know they just up and tell you they're leaving with no rhyme or reason? Sounds pretty suddenly to me."

"Well I can't answer for her."

"I'm not asking you to. I'm just saying it still doesn't compute. People don't just share a room with someone and then suddenly up and leave for no reason. Especially without saying a word." He hooked the pen onto his clipboard.

"I have no idea, sir. It's just been a few days I been here myself."

"When?"

"Bout a week or two. I'm just trying to get back on my feet, then

I'm out - so I didn't really get a chance to know her all that well." She folded her hands across her lap patiently, trying to still her nerves as she watched him scribble down more information.

"Thank you for your time." He stood and shook her hand then left.

*****

Carlotta poured the last of the drink into her glass and watched the man disappear into the bathroom... It would only be a matter of time, she reminded herself then checked her reflection in the mirror.

"Relax, you look beautiful." The tall handsome gentleman eased up behind her, gently wrapping his strong rugged hands around her tiny waist.

"Thankyou." She followed him to the small corner table in the tiny hotel room as they sat down to finish their cocktails. "And you are very handsome." She smiled demurely as she watched him chug down the last of his drink and pick up the remote.

"Thanks babe." He yawned, flipping from channel to channel.

"Sleepy?" She scooted closer, placing her hand on his shoulder, gently massaging away the pressure as she watched him fade in and out.

"You really got the touch babe, you know?" He leaned forward and collapsed.

"Just relax." She reached into the bucket and filled the napkin with ice and pressed it to the back of his head as he lay snoring, then picked up his wallet.

*****

Vicky dumped the heavy wheelbarrow of scrap metal into the electric furnace of molten steel nearly plunging over the deck into the firey melting pot as she stumbled backwards and hit the floor barely escaping the fall. She could feel the energy slowly draining from her body as she reached for the ramp banister and staggered forward and hit the ground again...

"Too much of a liability, sorry gotta let you go." She could hear the distant voice of the department manager fading in and out as he walked to the door in the back office of the steel mill and held it open. The streets were drab and empty as she headed towards the train station, her mind racing back to the last scuffle when Anita tried to clobber her. Going back to the shelter wasn't even a thought.

"No loitering ma'am." The transportation attendant appeared.

"I'm homeless." Her eyes filled with tears as she looked up at his blurry image.

"Sorry, but it's the rules. You can't just sit here unless you're planning to ride."

"I just got fired I didn't even get no paycheck."

"These are the breaks, but you can't sit here." He reached out his hand and helped her to her feet as she headed to the turn-style into the night. The evening sky was pitch black as she brushed away the tears with the back of her sleeve and headed down the empty streets toward the local dive and peered through the windows into the eclectic ambiance as the jovial patrons of the after-work crew toasted up and mixed and mingled.

A soft glare from the local deli across the way cast a murky glow onto the pavement as she made her way across the avenue to the small convenience store then crept inside and snuck down the neatly lined snack aisle. Quickly stealing a quick glance over her shoulder, she scanned her options then grabbed a mini-pack of double stuffed oreos and stashed them into her hobo bag and tipped toward the cooler section. Again checking the coast was clear, she opened the door and reached inside scoring three beers and a couple whiskey sour wine coolers, then moved toward the exit and disappeared into the night.

A scarce group of people peppered the murky boulevard as she cut a corner and followed the winding trail to the park and sat down on a bench, then reached inside and pulled out the bottles and turned up, guzzling them down one by one as she curled up on the bench and dozed off. The pain and the struggle disappearing as her tensions slowly faded away as she drifted further and further from reality.

"*The park is closed*???" The words reverberated in her head as she jerked forward and sat up, startled by the familiar voice.

"I fell asleep." Vicky rubbed her eyes and focused on the blurry vision standing over her.

"Hey, you okay?" Ralph leaned over and placed his arm around her shoulder and sat down on the bench beside Vicky.

"It's too much." She looked down in despair.

"But it's okay kid." He reached for her hand, gently helping her up as he led her toward the car. "I got you."

"Where we goin?" She followed reluctantly.

"Didn't I just say *I got you*?" He pulled out the key fob and opened the door. "Just relax."

"Forgive me for asking, but it's not everyday I just up and go hoppin' into random cars with people I don't know, ya know?" She slid in cautiously as she watched the tall muscular frame close the door then walked around to the other side and climb behind the wheel.

"Girl you better quit playin', you know you just saw me at the shelter." He reached into the glove compartment and handed her a tissue then started the car. "Let's get you warmed up a bit."

"Thanks." She dabbed around the corners of her eyes.

"No problem..." He glanced into the rear view mirror at her weary appearance. "So how's life treating you these days?"

"Isn't it obvious?" She dropped her head and looked down in embarrassment at the tattered rags and torn up jeans as the tears began to roll.

"Hey, don't do that..." He handed her some extra tissue then reached for her hand and held it a moment. "Hang in there kid. Last time I saw you – thought you were looking into that position we talked about."

"Too hard, I guess I just couldn't cut the mustard."

"That's crazy." He adjusted his car seat and folded his arms across his chest. "Yeah, it can get pretty rough over there from time to time."

"And that's putting it nicely. But thanks anyway, I was hoping it worked out so I could have saved up enough for a place to finally call my own."

"Way to go." He gave the air a fist pump.

"It was until I accidentally almost fell over into the scrap metal fire pit when I was trying to dump a wheel barrow, that's when I finally came to my senses."

"Yikes.."

"Exactly."

"I take it that didn't go over too well."

"Good guess. They claimed I was too much of a potential liability to risk a chance on me and suggested I look into a different career path."

"*Gotcha.*" He pulled off his cap and ran his fingers through his buzz cut. "Well, technically it's my lunch break, but I just so happened to be taking a walk through the park just to catch some fresh air and I noticed you lying out there on the bench so I thought I'd check onya and see what's goin on. I always be tryna to keep an eye out, lend a helping hand when I can or wherever I sense a need. Don't even gotta rise to the occasion of a emergency. If I can help somebody out - I will. Ain't nothing wrong with goin' the extra mile - that's what's wrong with the world today. Nobody don't wanna help *nobody* out."

"Thats very kind of you, and rare."

"I mean, I ain't never went this far, I try to respect people's privacy but something told me to check on you because you don't exactly fit the profile or look like the type that belongs out here in these streets, especially on no park bench if you catch my drift. Or in no dang on shelter for that matter."

"I catch it and I get it, but I been on my own since I was twelve years old. Unfortunately in my life I never really had a choice."

"Twelve years old? Unbelievable."

"Yeah, unfortunately it is."

"But why?"

"Looong story."

"No family and friends you can call on?"

"Let's just say I got abandoned early in life - for different reasons."

"*Tragic*." He looked out the window in deep thought.

"Either way it go, I can't go back to that shelter it's just not safe."

"And you think these streets are safer?"

"Let's just say I'll take my chances."

"Wow if it's that serious up in there, we need to do whatever it is *they're* doin' and we could probably clean up these streets - if that's the case. Still in all, you *think* it's wild in there - but this out here is most definitely a jungle and seriously not the answer... Ain't no telling what will or can happen to you at any given time. It's only a *matter* of time."

"I know."

"How old are you?" He surveyed her long platted braids.

"How old do I look?"

"Early to mid-twenties I'd say."

"Twenty one. And you?"

"Me what?"

"Quit playing, how old are *you*?"

"Let's just say I'm a whole lot older than twenty one, I'll tell ya that much."

"So how long you been on the force?"

"Long enough to know you don't belong out here. Look, I would really hate to see you run into a situation or something happen to you out here in these streets - come on it gotta be someone you can call on. No family or friends?"

"Nope."

"Okay, I got an idea – let me see if I can reach out to some people who might have some connections with some folks at the "Young Adults - At Risk" program who might be able to get you hooked up with a job and maybe a rental room or something." He reached into the console and pulled out a card and scribbled on the back. "Give these folks a call and tell 'em Ralph sent you. I also work in conjunction with various judicial programs for the at-risk population, juveniles, adults and the Homeless Prevention Team. They will know me by my last name, O'Brien."

"Thank you so much for everything, sir."

"No problem. And I'll check back with them on my end to see if they heard anything or not, we gotta get you off these streets as soon as possible. To be honest, sometimes in life we gotta hunker down and do alotta things we might not wanna do, especially when it's in our own best interest in the long run. So you just may wanna consider going back to that shelter, at least for a couple nights, as opposed to sleeping out here on park benches or wherever. At least you'll have a roof over your head for the time being. I know it might not be the most desirable of circumstances you could wish for - especially considering some of the people you gotta interact with in there, like those bullies you mentioned or that wonderful roommate of yours... But in the long run, you still have some form of stability and a pinch of protection - at least until you can get back up on your feet, that is."

"True."

"Speaking of roommate..." He glanced at his watch. "When's the last time you seen her, what's her name Carlotta?"

"I haven't."

"I'm sure you're not complaining, given the problems you two have had. Anyway, looks like my break time is just about over. But like I said, you hang in there young lady. Sometimes we run into struggles outside of our control with no way out it seems. But you just have to keep the faith, stay strong and watch the people you associate with so you or they, don't block your blessings. Pay attention to that inner-voice. And *Listen* to it. Our Creator instilled it in us for a reason."

"I do try, but it's hard sometimes."

"HE never said it would be easy, but it's definitely worth it. Most of the time the right way is usually the hardest, that's why it's called *The Road Less Traveled.* Definitely ain't no cake walk, but we have to be of good courage. I'm not saying life won't throw you some curveballs, because it most definitely will, but when it comes down to the basic fundamentals of life - it's a lot more simple than we as humans give it credit for.

Mankind as a whole, tends to make things a lot more complicated than they actually are and often concentrate on what looks unchangeable instead of working hard on what is. Which could save folks a whole lotta agony in the end. Three of life's biggest lessons; don't sweat the small stuff, being wise works just as good as being strong because it can help us to avoid some of the pitfalls and snares that drain our strength... And last but not least, *When you don't understand His hand, humble yourself and trust His Heart.* Be safe. My cell number's on the back of the card."

"You as well...*And Thank you Ralph.*" Vicky felt an unusual rush of relief as she climbed out of the black Riviera and waved goodbye...

*****

Ralph watched from a distance as young buck mumbled to himself combing the aisles, dressed in rags. He could tell by the lost look in his eyes that something just wasn't right as he followed him through the store before the husky bodyguard accosted him, slamming him to the floor followed by a team of security guards.

"Hey, let 'em up man, he's just a kid." He ran to the juvenile's defense and intervened, reaching down to help the youngster up.

"Get back unless you wanna go down with him!" The burly watchman shouted and reached for his tazer as the young man squealed to the top of his lungs, writhing back and forth trying to break free as he shuddered in convulsions.

"Look, I told you to let him go, I'm his uncle." Ralph pleaded, his heart skipping a beat as he watched the adolescent struggle, begging for them to release the ruthless chokehold.

"Listen, we've already received several calls. Shoplifting is willful theft and this is a Class 1 Misdemeanor - now get outta my way or you're going down with him."

"I'm not even worried about it because for starters you have nothing on me or no reasoning to take me down. And plus you're not even the police, so you're really not about to arrest anyone." He squared up with the guard like it was his own son, attempting to reason. "Look, what does he have and how much does it cost?" Ralph reached into the young man's back pocket and pulled out a pack of cookies. "Come on man, all this over a few graham crackers? It ain't even worth it." Ralph pulled out his wallet and took out a five-dollar bill. "I got it man - where's the checkout?"

"That's not the point, sir." The guard eased up his grip and met Ralph face to face. "Theft is larceny and he broke the law. Period."

"Look, check it out man." He glanced at young buck then back at the gaurd. "You can plainly see he's going through something right? Now, what if it was your son or nephew or family member? Hey, I may not know what his issue is but you can look at him and tell there's definitely something going on. Seriously, why not just go on ahead and let me pay it forward, ya know?" Ralph reasoned, then pulled out his card and handed it to the guard.

"Oh, you're with the Young Adult-Risk Program - I believe we've got a contract with them. You guys do great work throughout the community." His demeanor quickly shifted as he reached out for a handshake.

"Awe thanks. Yeah, it takes a village right?" Ralph gave him a fist pump then leaned over and helped the young man up.

"Look, I don't know what's come over me and I usually don't do this but I'm gonna make an exception this one time. Now I can't promise you the next time..."

"Hey, ain't gonna be no next time, right champ?" Ralph glanced at the young man as he nodded innocently. "Cool. Hey, good lookin' out my man, God bless." He placed his arm around the young man's shoulder then handed the guard the money.

"I got it." The security officer shoved away the bill then took the pack of cookies to the small self checkout machine and swiped it with his ID then handed it back.

"Thanks for workin' with me man." Ralph nodded at the guard then led the young man out the store and handed him the snack. "So what's goin' on young homie?"

"'Preciate it. I'm just sayin' though...it's rough out here." He ripped open the package and shoved three cookies in his mouth. "I'm just goin' through a real rough time. On the real."

"Hey, it was just about to get a whole lot rougher - you was just about to go to jail back there, youngin."

"I do recognize that fact and I so appreciate you havin' my back, I just be feeling like ain't nobody trying to hear me. You know, like don't nobody really understand. Almost like I don't deserve no respect but I'm like how is that when I feel like I deserve all the respect in the world for what I already survived."

"I get that, but you know you're not the only one goin' through something, right? This is life, youngster."

"But it's like whenever I do try to do good nobody acknowledges it and everybody tries to run all over me and take advantage, forcing me to stand up for myself. Then when I do, I always end up in trouble. It's like a no-win game. Then it's like don't nobody even recognize my struggle...It's crazy, man. I just be feelin' like I gotta get it how I live."

"Yeah, but I hate to see you throw your life away over a package of cookies, though....or any reason for that matter. You look like and *sound* like you might have a pretty good head on your shoulders if you just focus and stay out the way."

"That sound like nerd talk to me."

"Hey, believe it or not - I used to be like you when I was young."

"Get out." The young man looked Ralph up and down then shook his head.

"Seriously though, I might look all buttoned up and square right now, but I paid my dues."

"Yeah, okay..."

"Seriously. It may not look like it, but I been around the block myself a time or two."

"Straight- what time was that?"

"Just trust me when I tell you - I been there..."

"Awww okay, so it must of been before I was born or somethin' like that."

"Well it definitely wasn't after." Ralph snickered. "What's your name son?"

"Timothy." He shifted his gaze.

"Cool, I'm Ralph. How old are you, by the way."

"Eighteen."

"Shouldn't you be in school right about now?"

"I got kicked out."

"And why is that?"

"They was trippin'."

"Oh really?"

"Seriously...all cause I missed a couple days."

"Truancy?"

"Whatever they call it."

"Only a couple?"

"I mean... give or take. They don't be talkin' about nothin' - like any of that stuff is really gonna help somebody in life. Please, miss me with that."

"Sorry to burst your bubble, son, but without a skill set you're gonna end up right where you are right now. Back out on the streets."

"And? I know tons of street hustlers and they're all ballin'." Timothy waved his hand in the air and rolled his eyes.

"So it seems. At least for now, anyway. You don't know what lies ahead for them - that route always ends in destruction." Ralph warned.

"Please, I witnessed alotta adults goin' to work everyday working so hard and they end up losing their house, car - everything. It don't pay to be good in this world and I'm a young cat and I can even see it."

"That's because the road to true abundance and life is narrow and few, very few people ascribe to it."

"Cause they know it ain't goin' nowhere, that's why." Timothy challenged.

"Come on, you gotta do better than that. You don't wanna let your parents down."

"What parents?" He dropped his head.

"It's okay." Ralph patted him on the shoulder and gave him a fatherly nudge.

"You aight for a old dude, you know?" He straightened his shoulders and shook it off.

"Actually, I didn't recognize I was that old til you brought it up, but thanks anyway...I think." Ralph stifled a giggle.

"Can I let you in on a secret?" Timothy looked up in the sky for a moment then back at the ground.

"Hey, I'm all ears."

"Sometimes I be hearin' voices, man. No joke." He placed his hands over his face and leaned against the brick wall outside the exit of the grocery mart. "And I can't get 'em to go away man, they just won't... It's crazy." He rubbed his temples and shook his head from side to side. "Nobody ever even tries to understand what I'm saying."

"I'm sorry to hear that young fella and I wanna help you, but I just need little more information - where are you staying?"

"I'm at my cousin's." He pointed. "It's over East."

"Let's go." Ralph headed toward the car and followed directions as he pulled in front of the small white wooden frame shack with chipped paint.

"Right here." Timothy pointed at the raggedy house.

"You good?" Ralph pulled over and paused for a minute as the young man nodded his head then hopped out the car as they headed to the front door.

"I guess." The young man shrugged his shoulders then rang the bell and waited patiently as an older man with grey hair appeared.

"Boy, where you been?" A look of concern crossed his face as he reached out and pulled the young buck close, wrapping his arms around him then quickly glanced at Ralph.

"Good to meet you, I run the Young Adult At-Risk Program downtown and I saw your cousin at the Grocery Mart just about to get into trouble so I stepped in."

"Man listen, I can't thank you enough." He held open the door and took a few steps back. "I'm Big Mike by the way, come on in."

"Cool, I'm Ralph." He shook his hand and stepped inside the neatly furnished house. "You know I hate to see a young man like this throw his whole life away, especially at such a young age. He seems to have so much promise, just needs a little guidance that's all.

"What am I gonna do with you, boy?" He glared. "What you done went and got into now?"

"Ain't nothin', dude." Timothy brushed past and headed toward the kitchen.

"Ain't no nothin' up in here and what did I tell you about addressing me like that? I'm not your dude - homie or nothing else. It's Big Mike and that's all it is to it." He spoke over his shoulder then turned back to Ralph and motioned toward the couch. "Have a seat, man."

"Hey, no problem at all, it's pretty much what I do... I think he was probably just a little hungry. The whole thing was over a package of cookies, believe it or not."

"Don't nothin' shock me when it comes to this boy, I don't know what gets into that cousin of mine. I know one thang, he ain't gonna drive me crazy with him, that's for sure. He been having these issues all his life. Ever since he was a child. He ain't been right since his pops put him up for adoption after he separated from his momma and she turned to the street life. I'm telling you, some days I can't even get him to change his clothes. He'll put on the same outfit for a whole week. I have just about begged and pleaded with that boy over and over again to change his crazy ways but I just can't seem to get through to him." He looked out the window in defeat. "He got a closet full of clothes so it's not like he dooesn't have anything to wear. It's like he's just set in his ways. Like he lost his passion for life or somethin'."

"Wow, I'm sorry to hear that."

"Then he done sat up here and got kicked out of school for missing so many days - I don't know what to do about him at this point. I'm just stumped." He threw his hands in the air.

"I really hate to hear this, you don't think he's taking anything do you - if you don't mind me asking?"

"Not that I know of."

"Well, he did tell me he feels sad, but that's just between you and me." Ralph whispered.

"Now *this*, I'm aware of... Unfortunately." Big Mike sat down and studied the floor in distress.

"Is he getting any help, do you know?"

"I try my best to get help for that boy but it's hard for him to keep a routine, he won't take his medication, he won't go to therapy - it's just alot to deal with and I'm by myself here. My wife passed away three years ago and I'm struggling to get by as it is. Some days I don't know whether I'm coming or going."

"I'm praying for you, man." Ralph stood and gave him a manly embrace of encouragement.

"Thanks man. I'm just doing the best I can with what I can."

"And that's all we can do. He's just a few years younger than our intake program requirement, but I may be able to pull some strings and see what else we can do. Maybe check into some other resources and services I can possibly tap into to see if I can help that way. Give me your number and I'll get back to you soon as I can and don't hesitate to call if you need any additional assistance." Ralph handed him an extra card to write down his number.

"Thanks for real man, I really appreciate all this."

"Never a problem. Hey, this is what we do. You hang in there pal, Peace." Ralph headed back to his car.

Chapter 5

The angry wind whipped around the corner as they huddled together beneath the flimsy cardboard box, bristling against the elements from the undercurrent of vicious tides swept up from the remnants of the hurricane. The storm had ravaged everything in sight. Roxanne looked around at the entire area swamped in flood waters, scattered with debris and clutter floating atop the murky river of sewage that had risen to five feet in some areas.

They had no place to go. Roxanne fought back the tears as she glanced around at her four children shivering in the cold, nestled beneath the makeshift cover from tattered pieces of cardboard and empty plastic bags dug from the trash. It was a tough decision, but she knew she had to face it or they would be subjected to the dangers of street life for who knows how long and no one even cared. She reached over to her youngest and stroked his short curly hair as he lay next to her while throngs of people stepped over them like litter on the ground.

But she knew she had to fight. Even if every place was filled to capacity and rejected them due to the storm, there was still a small window of possibility if just one facility opened its doors, at least for the children. She would gladly sleep out on the streets as long as they were safe. She dried her tears and gathered up her strength as she woke them one by one and headed toward the local orphanage.

"Please, can I speak to someone." Roxanne rushed toward the receptionist as her children filed in one by one, her solemn voice void with emotion as she directed her children toward the sitting area.

"What seems to be the issue?" The thin woman in wire framed glasses spoke from behind the desk.

"I just can't take it anymore..." Roxanne whispered as she fought back the tears fighting to be strong in front of her children. "We're homeless sleeping on the streets and have nowhere to go - the storm destroyed all that was left. Our house and all our belongings are gone."

"Are there any relatives you may be able to get in contact with?"

"Basically, no. And I quit my job five years ago to take care of my mother so I inherited the house when she passed away and now it's totally underwater." She glanced over at her children stretched across the carpet. "It was all we had."

"Let me see if I can find someone, just a second." She pressed the intercom button and called for assistance.

"You rang?" A tall brown skinned woman dressed in a black paintsuit appeared in the doorway.

"I think she's looking for some type of emergency services." She nodded toward the caseworker, then reached for Roxanne's hands to comfort her as they followed the woman into the sitting area.

"We got displaced by the storm and now our home is totally submerged in water. Like I said, it wasn't much - just a four room single story shack I inherited from my mother after she passed away - but it was ours." She re-explained the horrific circumstances in desperation.

"Absolutely horrible, my heart goes out to you." A look of despair crossed the woman's face.

"We haven't eaten anything in days and every place I called before my phone died turned us down due to capacity limitations so we're literally out on the streets. I just want to get my babies to safety and food and shelter. Even if I gotta sleep on the streets.... I'll be okay."

"Hey, I get it. But do you realize that this is a Social Services center and that your children will more than likely be placed in an orphanage?"

"At this point I don't have a choice, as long as they're not on the streets... what else can I do? I'm desperate." Roxanne broke down in tears as the youngest child jumped up from the floor and ran to console his mother.

"It's okay mommy, please don't cry!" He threw his arms around her waist.

"Come with me." The woman opened the door as Roxanne assembled her children and led her into the back area then handed her a packet of paperwork to fill out.. "Are you sure you're okay?"

"I can't think right now." The room spun in circles as she signed the paperwork and turned to hug her children.

"You all know mommy loves you, right?" She hugged them one by one and sobbed.

"Yes.. We love you too, mommy!!!" A symphony of tiny voices chimed in unison from the tiny group of tear stained faces.

"I'll be back, I promise...." She slowly backed away.

"I love you, mommy!" The youngest one charged forward, begging her to stay.

"Hey, mommy's gotta find us a new place to stay, that isn't filled with water... I promise it won't be too long, I just need to make sure you all are safe, first."

"But what about you?" The oldest reached out and grabbed her arm as they tugged on her crying out.

"Mommy's gonna be okay..." She took a few steps back and fell into the wall as the intake worker helped her back into the front office.

"DON'T LEAVE US MOMMY!" The youngest bolted toward the door knocking down the case worker as another staff member restrained him.

"I LOVE YOU MY BABIES!!!" Her heart shattered in a million pieces as she headed out the door into the dreary evening and dipped through the deep puddles of standing water, then made her way back to the old vacant lot on the main boulevard and crawled beneath the cardboard boxes, slowly fading away.

*****

It was 7:30 AM and the dump truck was running late for a change as Ralph sifted through the dumpsters and searched the area collecting old tin cans at the last minute. It was a small side hustle but the little change it did bring came in handy, here and there. He reminded himself as he stashed an armful of aluminum cans into a plastic bag as a distant noise crept up from under the pile of boxes by the chain link fence.

"Who's there?" He took a few steps toward the huge cardboard pile and dug through a couple layers.

"My babies are gone..." A tiny voice whispered from the petite figure curled up in a bundle.

"Take my hand." He eased down and extended his arm as she grabbed his wrist, then helped the woman to her feet.

"My babies... I had to leave my babies... *I didn't wanna do it, but I had to.*" She fell back against the fence.

"I don't understand... what happened?"

"The flood washed away everything the storm didn't take with it." She shivered, rocking back and forth... "Wasn't nothing but a piece of house and some throwed together bricks and mortar shack - but at least it was *Mine*. I never had nothin' my whole entire life - and the second my hands got ahold of somethin' here come the world tryna take it away from me - get away from me!" She picked up a can and threw it at him as he dodged the object just in time.

"Hold up a minute, no need to get violent, Okay? I'm not the enemy. I'm trying to *help* you - not harm you."

"I don't even know what that means anymore." She cringed in deep despair.

"And why is that?"

"Don't nobody want me to have *nothin'*. I had to fight for my mama's house to keep it from being auctioned off by the Repo man - then when I finally do gain possession of it, seems like everybody is trying to make me lose it - and now this.. I'm just tired." She sat on the ground and cried like a baby. "I take one step forward then ten backwards. This world is wearing me out."

"I'm sorry you're going through all of this... won't you let me help you?" He took another step forward.

"Get away!" She flailed her arms back and forth.

"I can *still* help you." He pleaded with compassion. "Just trust me..."

"And what makes you so special that I should trust you?"

"Just give me a chance."

"Yeah right - you probably had it good your whole entire life."

"Not true..." Ralph attempted to reason.

"Yeah okay... and where were you when my mother needed an emergency surgery and her insurance wouldn't cover it?"

"I'm sorry..."

"Where were you when she needed blood transfusions and a donor, but the waiting list was so long and all the red tape cost her-her life?"

"Again. I'm sorry you had to go through all that and I know I cannot change the past but if you will allow me to help you now - maybe I can help change the direction of your future..."

"How??? What you got, some magic potion or a new age wand stick- who are you supposed to be, anyway?"

"I come in peace..." He reached out his hand and gently helped her to her feet.

"I hate my life!!!" She screamed to the top of her lungs as she stood, slightly hunched over from the pain of lying on the cold hard concrete, night after night.

"It only takes the faith of a mustard seed... Will you follow me?.." He took her arm and gently guided her toward his car.

"Where are you taking me, how do I know you're not crazy?" She froze in the middle of the streets for a moment.

"Trust me, crazy people don't put their life on the line offering assistance to people in need, with nothing to gain."

"So what you got on it?"

"Excuse me?"

"Laymen's terms... what you got on it?"

"LOVE."

"Who?"

"Will you follow me?" He continued toward the car as she reluctantly trailed behind.

"Where we goin?"

"A far better place than sleeping on the cold hard concrete." He held open the door as she climbed inside then pulled out a plastic bag filled with snacks.

"Don't mind if I do." She reached inside with both hands and pulled out several bags of chips then stuffed them into the side pockets of the oversized overcoat.

"Think you got enough?" He glanced at the half empty sack and smirked.

"For the time being." Vicky snickered then popped open a bag and devoured it.

*****

"She may be too old for this program and you know it." The head coordinator stared at Ralph in confusion. "You keep bringing people in here that don't match the intake criteria and you know as well as I do - how the program works because you run it - so what gives???"

"Life???"

"Come on man, there you go getting all psychoanalytical on me."

"Would you rather her sleep on the concrete by the garbage barrels until you read about it in the news. This woman had to sign her children into an orphanage because their house is covered in water - would you like to move in there? Or better yet, curl up beside a garbage dumpster every night and brave the elements of who knows what and risk your life?"

"And you're trying to save the world or what?"

"My question to you is, why are you *not* trying to help save it - or at least help those you can along the way. You never know when you might need some assistance yourself, one day." Ralph stared him straight in the eye.

"Look man.. I just came to do my job."

"Which brings to me my next question, why sign up for a job to help people in need if you don't have the compassion it takes to help the people in need??"

"What's this supposed to be, some type of quiz?"

"It's more like a heart-assessment... An internal investigation of your moral code... ethics and integrity." Ralph countered.

"Look, I'm not here to debate or one-up you on who's the better man for the job. After all - if you think I'm not fit why did you even hire me in the first place? Matter fact, you are welcome to un-hire me right now at any given moment because apparently I don't have what it takes according to your high code of ethics."

"Come on, it's not about one-upping or debating anything. It's about coming together for the common good of us all. Mankind as a whole no matter who you are. And I hired you to do a job because I wanted to help you out since you yourself needed a job or you couldn't pay your rent and didn't have a place to stay, remember?" Ralph reiterated.

"Yeah..." He dropped his gaze to the floor.

"And in turn, you're helping others who are also in need...see how it works?"

"You right man, I stand correcting. I do apologize." The worker expressed his regret.

"No need - all I ask is one favor."

"I'm listening..."

"Get her signed up, a cot and a fresh meal and temporary room and board in one of the rooms with the other older residents who are here on a temporary basis, until I find a conducive placement. The Salvation is filled to capacity due to the storm."

"Got it." He grabbed the paperwork and headed into the lobby to assist the woman.

Chapter 6

"It's all yours." Roscoe, the store manager, handed Vicky the keys to the gas station.

"I can never thank you and Ralph enough." Vicky tried to fight back the tears as she reached for the keys. It had been a long time since anyone had shown her any amount of kindness. It was like the entire world was against her and there was no way out.

"I've gotta admit, Ralph's definitely one of the good ones for sure. He goes out of his way helping people get back on their feet all the time. He's like an angel in disguise, I like to say. Hey, you gonna be alright?" He noticed her emotional state as he reached out to stroke her arm.

"It's just been really hard lately." She wiped her face with the back of her hand, then looked around the stockroom filled with boxes as a group of men climbed off the truck lift and began unpacking a fresh new load of items.

"I hear ya." He tapped her on the shoulder. "Hey, don't feel like you gotta get everything done tonight, I got this." He glanced over at the incoming boxes. "You just focus on the register and after you shut down, go on and head on over across the lot to Budget Suites and they'll show you your room. I've already given them a heads up so they know you're a part of the Young Adult Risk Program. They also have a contract with us. We'll have you back up and running in no time, you just hang on in there - and don't give up the faith." He reassured as he headed out the door then hopped inside his silver Jaguar and sped off.

The gas station was empty and the traffic on the street was light as Vicky damp mopped the floor with bleach and finished stocking the last shelves when the door sensor chimed. "Sorry, I'm just about to close." Vicky looked up from her evening chores as a dark figure flashed in the corner of her eye. "May I help you?" She focused on the medium framed individual dressed in a saddle brown coat and dark blue jeans.

"I was just checking to see was y'all was hiring?" A low toned voice escaped from a pair of ruby red lips of the hidden face, cloaked behind a black beanie and dark shades.

"I actually just started myself, what hours were you interested in?"

"Night shift."

"Cool, let me reach out to Roscoe and see if he might be able to hook you up, he's the store manager. Maybe I can put in a good word for you because I know what it's like when you're looking for work. Like I said, I just got on myself."

"Wonderful, in the mean and in-between, I'm out here starvin' like Marvin so can you perhaps hook me up with a bite to eat?" She gripped the jumble of keys and balled up her fist. "And possibly throw in a little extra change while you're at it?"

"I'm not sure I know what you mean." Vicky dropped the mop and took a few steps back.

"You heard me right... Let's make it snappy Miss Happy."

"Oh my gosh, is that *you*?" Vicky shrieked in terror as she recognized the familiar voice and the faint scent of Violets In Bloom body spray.

"In the flesh." Carlotta snickered beneath the masculine disguise.

"You do know they got cameras in here *right*?" Vicky quivered frozen in fear.

"And you do know I don't care about all that right?" Carlotta stepped forward, clutching the keychain defensively.

"Look, I don't want any trouble."

"*Who does*?" She snickered. "Quit playing, you know what time it is."

"Why are you harassing me?"

"Hunger?"

"Yeah, but why me?"

"Gullible?" Vicky laughed even louder.

"Look, a caseworker from the Department of Human Services stuck his neck out to get me this job."

"*And*?"

"Come on, I don't wanna blow it. What happened to you anyway, you just got up and left the shelter?" Vicky skillfuly diverted the conversation.

"Yeah, I had to hit the gas on that joint."

"Well, someone came looking for you."

"What can I say, folks just love me like that, I guess." Carlotta snarled arrogantly.

"I wouldn't get too excited, it was a caseworker."

"So you ratted me out?" She peered over the black shades.

"Noooo.... I just told him I was only in there a few weeks and never even really got to know you."

"Good lookin' out, I raised you well, I see. You make me proud you know that right?"

"Please don't do this. Seriously, it's not even worth it." Vicky rationalized.

"Really?"

"Really. There's so much more life has to offer you if you just give it half a chance."

"And who are you, the spokesperson for the lost? Just like the straight-laced, goody two shoes you are, always playing by the rules. Don't make me laugh. Just curious though, how's that been working out for ya so far?" Carlotta chuckled, spinning the key ring around her finger.

"You're welcome to put those away anytime, you know."

"I'll be the judge of that."

"I'm just saying, there's always a better way..."

"You can keep your advice. You could never even possibly relate to my situation - all your life you had it easy. You have NO idea what it's like to struggle, so you can keep the corny words of encouragement and just give up the cash."

"I'm just saying, we all have our struggles... even me."

"Oh really? Don't tell me, you ran out of icing one day when you were making your favorite brownies and had to make a mad dash to the grocery store. Please save the sob stories."

"I'm just speaking facts. You are a beautiful queen with your whole life ahead of you. You should never have to resort to something like this."

"How touching. What can I say, you got me on the verge of tears." Carlotta bit down on her bottom lip and let out a snarl.

"Seriously, I don't want any trouble." Vicky dried her tears with the back of her sleeve.

"Good, me either. Now hurry up and clean out that register so I can be on my merry little way. Or else. And I wouldn't think about pressing that panic button under the counter either if I was you, just in case it happened to cross your mind. It probably won't work out too well for ya sweetie." Carlotta shoved Vicky toward the checkout counter and watched her open the register as she pulled out a stack of cash. Then snatched the money and dashed out the door, disappearing into the night.

The cool brisk air of the autumn breeze against her skin stilled her nerves as she dipped through a walkway and cut down the dark alley. Quickly snatching off the knitted beanie, she pulled the rubberband from her hair releasing her long locks then tossed the shades as the sound of sirens filled the air. There had to be a way out, she rationalized, hurriedly ripping off her coat and unzipping her pants as she stripped down to a pair of leggings. Then discarded the denim slacks into a nearby dumpster and scanned the murky premises.

She never wanted it to be this way, but it had to be. Her mind raced as she considered her options, then quickly hopped the fence and headed in the opposite direction of the piercing alarm. People were too mean and cruel, always taking advantage...there was nowhere else to go and life had been too hard. The random thoughts plagued her mind as she fought to compose herself and justify her conscious for the wrong she had done. But it was all she knew to do in order to survive life, the streets and the jungle.

*****

"*Help me please!!!*" Vicky screamed out in distress as a customer stepped inside and knelt down to comfort her.

"What's going on?" He placed his arm around her neck.

"Somebody came in and demanded me to empty the register." Vicky shuddered in distress.

"Calm down, you're okay - when did all this happen???"

"Just a few minutes ago." She trembled uncontrollably.

"What's goin' on?" Ralph stepped inside, followed by Roscoe the store manager.

"Oh my gosh, you just missed it."

"Missed what?" Ralph leaned over and helped Vicky up.

"It was only about five minutes ago." She covered her face with her hands in despair.

"It's alright, I'm here." The officer glanced at Roscoe as he stroked Vicky's shoulder then pulled her into his arms and held her tight. "You really need to file a report young lady so we can catch this joker. I know you're pretty nervous right now but if you could give us a description it'd be great."

"I don't remember."

"Excuse me?" He leaned back for a moment, puzzled by her response.

"Maybe you just didn't understand the question. I'm asking if the suspect was male or female?"

"All I remember is a pair of blue jeans and a brown jacket." She dropped her head and quickly looked away.

"But you still can't say whether it was a man or a woman?"

"*Nooo.*" She weeped.

"First time I heard that one."

"They had on some type of disguise."

"What do you mean a disguise."

"I mean... I couldn't see their face behind the shades and the hat. You came just in the knick of time." Vicky turned to Ralph and gave him a big hug.

"You're okay." He stroked her arm. "What an astonishing coincidence, I usually come up here a couple times a week around this time just to touch base with my buddy Roscoe." He grabbed Vicky's hand and headed toward the door. "Come on, you're comin' with me." He stopped and glanced at Roscoe. "You good, or you need me to stick around for a few?"

"I think I can handle it from here, just take care of our girl." Roscoe nodded at Vicky reassuringly.

"I got her." Ralph grabbed her hand and led her to his car then headed toward the motel.

"You know, it really saddens me to see something like this happen to someone like you. Especially after all of the hard work you've put into the program. You're a good person and this was your opportunity to finally get off these streets and turn your life around. I really feel for you. I work with a lot of young adults and it isn't every day that I see the level of determination and commitment that matches yours. I see a lot of potential in you, young lady. Keep up the good work, keep thriving and don't let this mean old world stop you."

"Thank you for everything." A trail of tears streamed down her face as she leaned on his shoulder for support.

"Tell ya what." Ralph studied the floor for a second in deep thought. "Let me see if I can pull some more strings with the folks down at the Young Adult Program, but until then, first things first." He grabbed her hand and helped her out of the car. "Let's get you back to your room and situated so you can rest up. Don't stress, I'll notify the folks over at the motel that there's been a change in plans for the time being and we'll see what we can do from there.... Deal?" He pulled a tissue from his shirt pocket and wiped away her tears.

"Deal." She whispered, feeling safe for the first time in her life.

"I wanna share something with you, but first you gotta make me a promise." He pulled off the service cap and smoothed down his course hair, then he grabbed the handle and held open the door.

"I promise." Vicky agreed instantly as she stepped into the building.

"Now I want you to listen to me and listen very carefully... and you must never forget what I'm about to tell you."

"I won't."

"In this life, you're gonna cross paths with all types of people. It's inevitable, that's just the way it is. And not all of them will have your best interest at heart, which I'm pretty sure you've already figured that out by now. In this life, you will face a lot of hard times, ups and downs. Situations will come at you and there's no way you will ever be able to pull out of it or overcome them unless you have one thing. Any idea what that is?"

"Strength?"

"This is beyond your own strength. This right here is a call of faith. You have to learn to reach deep inside yourself and pull it out... Don't be afraid to lean on it because in this world... that's all you truly have in the end. Without faith there is no way you can withstand the harsh realities of this world or overcome the blows of this life. Some people will test you in all walks of life and without reason or cause."

"But it just feels so undeserved - I did nothing to her..."

"So you've finally confessed."

"Confessed to what?"

"Just a few minutes ago, when we were talking to the store manager back there, you said it was hard to tell if the person was male or female due to a disguise... and now you just admitted that it was, in fact, a female when you made reference about having done nothing to provoke her betrayal - whether or not you realize it. Look, I know these streets young lady...*I'm from these streets*." Ralph pounded his chest. "Which also leads me to believe you may know a lot more about this person than you're willing to admit. It's something you're not telling me."

"I promise I'm not hiding anything, sir. I just recognized the flowery cologne and that's what made me think it was a female."

"Oh you *recognized*...That's quite an interesting choice of words, wouldn't you say? In order for you to recognize something it has to be familiar to you. There has to have been some prior form of contact - who do you think you're talking to???"

"Like I said, I noticed the cologne because I also have the fragrance and I just don't think a male would wear something like that."

"Yeah right. Look, I wanna believe your story. I really do. But unfortunately....I just don't. On the real. Either way, in regard to my previous statement, I do acknowledge the dismal reality of this world and the fact that every offense is not always provoked. The world is overwhelmed with agitators and instigators. It's deeply fallen. Troubled with all kinds of contagious diseases, from malice and vengeance to deception and greed - you name it." He pulled into the motel parking lot. "Well, here we are young lady."

"Do I just go in?" Vicky peered through the motel lobby entrance door hesitantly.

"Tell you what, gimme a second and I'll be right back."

"Okay." Vicky watched as Ralph stepped outside the car and pulled out his cell phone. "*It's all over now...*" Wicked thoughts filled her head as she fought to contain herself. Her entire body a complete sack of nerves as she trembled uncontrollably, reminiscing over the pain in her life. Rock bottom had finally come. She peeped out the tinted window of the black Riviera. "*What was the point, anyway?*" She wondered hopelessly. Everything was gone now and the shelter was too dangerous. They would be sure to eradicate her if she ever went back there, but the streets were no one's friend either and she knew that....She dropped her head, attempting to process the negative thoughts. Then jerked forward, startled by the loud knocking sound jolting her back to reality.

"Hey, didn't I tell you I was plugged?" Ralph tapped on the window and broke through the silence as he opened the back door and helped her out, then led her inside the building. "Genevieve, this here is my friend Vicky." He held her hand as he introduced her. "She's a bit down on her luck right now, but with a little prayer and support we're gonna get her straightened out just right. All she needs is a helping hand and some tender lovin' care... so I brought her on over cause I figured you wouldn't mind maybe helping her out some. She's in the Young Adult Risk Program and we had her lined up with a clerk position but things are kind of shaky over there at the gas station right now - so I'm just wondering could we help her out. Keep her safe and outta trouble." He glanced at the front desk clerk and winked.

"Sorry to hear that, yes I heard what happened and I'm so glad you are safe...I'm sure we can pitch in and find something." The heavy set woman came from around the front desk and embraced her for a moment. "It's okay, dear."

"I have nowhere to go. I was staying at the shelter but..."

"No worries hun, there's no need to explain. We have a dishwashing position, if you don't mind doing that type of work?" She waved at Ralph and headed up the stairs. "I can take it from here."

"I'm open to anything, as long as I don't have to go back there..." Vicky struggled to hold back a fresh barrage of tears as she followed the woman up the long flight of stairs.

"It's okay. We work very closely with the Young Adult Program doing all we can to keep our young people off the streets... and really anybody who needs help." She turned down a long corridor and headed toward a small room in the back. "This is a single bed but it should suffice for the time being."

"It's actually very charming." Vicky stepped inside the cozy little twin bed space with a small bathroom and a beautiful window view of the boulevard.

"There's some clean linen, other basic necessities and a care package with some hygiene products." The kind woman picked up a pair of uniform scrubs and handed them to her. "The hospital also donates these."

"But how do I cover my room and board, will the kitchen position take care of the expenses? I have nothing to my name."

"That's a good question sweetie, you're on a roll." The woman chuckled. "Actually we also get funding through certain government programs and a variety of different resources. Most of our residents become employed either at this facility or any of our affiliate work programs. Follow me." She headed back into the hallway and down the stairs toward the back entrance of the huge industrial kitchen and handed her an apron.

"But I don't have any experience..."

"We definitely got you covered. The job is relatively self explanatory and there are easy-to-read instruction manuals on all of the equipment, but staff is always willing to help out if you need anything.

We like to keep it nice and simple with as least amount of stress as possible. You've already been through enough. The training consists of operational instructions and cleaning duties for our large industrial equipment dishwashers and sanitizing machinery. You will be paid weekly one hundred dollars, which half will automatically go toward your room and board, meals are free and if everything works out you are good to go. Any questions?" Genevieve smiled encouragingly.

"I think I can handle it." Vicky looked around the huge commercial kitchen and spotless floor in admiration. It was a far cry compared to what she had come from.

"Oh, and I almost forgot..." She reached inside her frock and pulled out a tiny reloadable flip phone. "It comes with three hundred minutes for twenty dollars a month as long as you're in our work program. The expense is automatically deducted from your pay but at least you do have something. We like to try and provide as much help as we can to get and keep our young adults safe and set them on the path of a fresh new start. The long-term goal is to stick out the program until you complete some type of job training skill such as waitress, cook, data entry... There's a whole list of options to choose from but the role of the program is to get you headed in the right direction so that you can attain gainful employment, get into your own place and lead an independent life on your own..."

"God bless you." Vicky squeezed the kind woman and balled her eyes out as she headed to her workstation with a renewed sense of peace, then loaded the rest of the dishes into the heavy-duty dishwasher and followed the instructions on the door. It may not have been someone else's dream job but it was way better than living on the streets from pillow to post. She reconciled herself as she picked up the mop and fed it through the mechanical bucket, then pulled it through the rollers and wrung it out as she stretched to relieve her aching muscles.

"You good?" The supervisor returned a few hours later.

"I need a break."

"You have my permission, go ahead and do you."

"Thanks." Vicky gave a quick nod and headed through the swinging exit doors as an unseen gust of force slammed her into the concrete wall.

"So you finally made it big, hey?" Carlotta snickered as she snaked her from behind.

"Why are you following me?!?" Vicky screeched, engulfed in fear.

"Awww...Thought you got away, didn't you? I can't believe you actually thought I'd leave without a proper farewell. Come on you know me better than that." Carlotta whispered from behind, her voice filled with vengeance as she forced her hand into Vicky's pockets and emptied out the contents, quickly stashing them into her belt bag as she made a mad dash down the stairwell.

Chapter 7

The bright red fire engine roared down the main Boulevard followed by an ambulance as Ralph ran toward the old steel mill building, fighting his way through the intense crowd as everyone gazed in terror at the young man standing on the rooftop. His blurry image grew crystal clear as he recognized the youngster's face.

"DON'T DO IT..." The negotiator's voice blared over the PA System. "Just give me a chance... I promise I can help you, but you gotta believe in me though. Trust me, I won't turn my back on you but you gotta let me in first." His voice cracked with emotion as he tried to rationalize.

"Timothy, my man, what's goin' on Bro?" Ralph worked his way into the center of the crowd as he looked up to the top of the building. "Hey, can we at least talk about it so I can know what's goin' on and how I can help?"

"*I'M SICK AND TIRED OF TALKING!!!*" Timothy hollered down, then took another step closer to the edge of the roof.

"C'mon Bro, this ain't even you. You better than this - you got way more heart than this." Ralph attempted to reason.

"Mannn... *It's Whatever.*" Timothy looked down for a second then back up into the sky.

"That's what I'm sayin' Bro - whatever it is let's sit down and converse about it. But this right here ain't cool...I'm just sayin...whatever it is we can make it do what it do... come to some type of understanding about this thing called life."

"We may need a tactical unit." A uniformed detective spoke into his radio.

"Hey, hold up man, hold up." Ralph intervened. "Check it out - lemme see if I can get through to him, first?"

"Look - appreciate your concern and all, but we're trying to avoid a major catastrophe here, if that's okay with you." The official snapped back.

"We're on the same page, but what we also don't want is to aggravate the situation and make it worse than it has to be... OR possibly fatal. I've met this young man before." Ralph reasoned. "He's got a few issues."

"Well, that much we can assume because no sane person gets on top of a roof without the intention of taking the stairs back down, if you get my drift. And would it seem to me that he's already aggravated." The mediator clicked the button on his radio and resumed communicating with the authorities.

"Hey, do *you* know what is going on inside this young man's head?" Ralph asserted distraughtly.

"No, but I do know whatever it is it ain't good and that much we can both agree on or he wouldn't be standing on top of this building ready to call it a day - wouldn't you agree?" The official sneered as he glared out of the corner of his eye with a hostile stare.

"Look, I'm not about to go tit-for-tat with you at a crucial time like this, but I just might know a tad bit more about this youngster than you do. And I run the Young Adult Risk Program. I deal with troubled youth all the time." Ralph introduced himself.

"Good to meet you, but realistically, at this point how can you really help?"

"Who knows, maybe I can persuade him in another direction. Get in his head and see what's goin' on. It's worth a try, don't you think?"

"Yeah but who's got that kind of time?" The two men continued to debate as the chief fireman rushed through the crowd, motioning his crew as they rolled out the hook ladder connected to the truck.

"Hold up Chief - that just might be the last straw that breaks the camel's back and pushes him one more step closer to the ledge. He's already on the tip of the iceburg." Ralph countered. "None of us truly know where his head is at - we don't wanna piss him off either."

"Tell you what my man..." Ralph shouted up toward the top of the building. "How 'bout I meet you up there and we can chop it up for a few? Hey, I won't judge - you already know *I know*."

"Just chill dude... I ain't tryna hear all that." Timothy hollered back as he looked down at the pavement for a second in deep thought, then wiped the tears from his blurry eyes. "Ain't nobody trying to understand me."

"That's exactly what I'm trying to do if you would just let me." Come on baby, champs don't go out like that - you got too much heart for this - *You Got This*."

"I don't know man..." Timothy sat down and dangled his legs over the side of the building to collect his thoughts as the crowd gasped in horror.

"Come on man.... you ain't tryna do this." Ralph helped the others stack the ladder against the brick building and placed his foot on the first rung. "Trust me, I ain't judgin'. If you heard my story you'd realize you ain't never in this thing alone. Nobody got it easy Fam. I done been where you are, where you goin' *and* where you never been. I've seen it all. And I done also overcame it all... It ain't over 'til the man upstairs say it's over... *know that*." He took another step, then two more as he climbed steadily all the way to the top of the roof. "*I GOT YOU!*" He reached out and grabbed Timothy, hugging him with all his might as he rocked him back and forth, then led him toward the flap door and held it open as they entered the building and headed down the stairway to the main entrance.

"Let's Talk About It Bay-bee!!!" Ralph fist pumped Timothy's chest playfully as they exited the building into the cheering crowd, then escorted him to the ambulance.

"I'm sick of this life, man." Timothy slumped forward in defeat as he studied the vinyl flooring of the emergency vehicle.

"Trust me, I do understand and I get it. But you gotta fight this thing man. You gotta *slay* this dragon - don't let this dragon *slay you, Bro*. Life has a way of getting the best of all of us at times but only the strong survive, youngster. I mean, we still gotta endure some life lessons in order to build that inner-muscle, no matter how strong you start off.

That's just the way it is. But always remember, life is gonna test you no matter how strong you think you are or *who* you think you are. And it takes no prisoners, my friend."

"Well, I had enough of enduring." Timothy rubbed his forehead in exhaustion. "I'm tired."

"Aren't we all. Unfortunately though, that's just now how it works, pal." Ralph explained as he settled back in his seat unfazed by the tribulations of life. "See, you can be born a fighter but true warriors are made. Shaped in the battlefield from life's war wounds. You're definitely gonna take some hits though, young homie. And what happened to Big Cuz - the one whose house I took you to that time?"

"Big Cuz gone, man." Timothy fought back the tears as he looked away.

"What do you mean he's gone?"

"He passed away..." Timothy rocked back and forth, struggling to find peace. "Dude was all I had... it's crazy. He understood me when nobody else did or cared. Now what?... It's all bad..."

"I feel you partna. I dedinitely do. This life ain't nothin' easy."

"What am I to do now... I can't think straight...I can't...focus... I can't do anything."

"What happened to him, if it's not too personal."

"His heart gave out. He had been sick for a while though, but he always pulled out of it. Then two nights ago all of a sudden he kept saying he couldn't breathe. And then... I guess he just let go." Timothy burst into tears.

"You got this young homie. Now all you gotta do is lean on Big

Homie - God Almighty. Trust me, He'll pull you through. He *truly* understands, even when nobody else does. Why do you think I'm still here, foreal-foreal. Let Him fight your battles, bind up your wounds, unscramble the chaos in your mind and in your heart. He's the *Great Comforter Almighty*." Ralph closed his eyes for a moment on a quick mental break, pondering the ramifications of life as they rode to the hospital in deep silence. "Come on let's go inside and get you something to calm down... take a load off." He gathered up his strength. "I'ma be there with you all the way, don't even trip. We in this together, Youngster." He hopped out of the ambulance and led the way toward the emergency room entrance.

"It doesn't even matter anymore." Timothy leaned back in the medical recliner, his body limp and distraught as the nurse took his vitals. "It's all a game, anyway..." He swallowed the pills. "We're all just pawns."

"Are the two of you related?" The nurse glanced at Ralph in concern as she raised Timothy's sleeve and administered the sedative.

"I'm just a friend of the family you could say, but I run the *At Risk Youth Program* so I do anything in my power to help out wherever there's a need. I'll see what we can do, even if I need to tap into the Salvation for some support. Who knows, they may even have an opening or a spare room."

"Good, so he does have some place to go. You are such a gem... An angel in disguise." The nurse smiled in adoration as she shook Ralph's hand. "He should be fine after a few hours, just needs to get a little rest. He seems pretty drained."

"Yes he does. Hey, thanks for everything and do stay blessed." Ralph nodded as he helped Timothy out the door.

"Oh, do you need a ride back?" She followed them into the hallway.

"As a matter-of-fact, we do. I left my car so I could accompany him in the ambulance."

"Hold on, I'm going to find a way to arrange something so you guys can get back to your original destination, how's that?" She picked up the hospital phone and dialed the receptionist then directed them past the lobby out into the parking lot as they climbed into a rideshare and headed back toward the main Boulevard.

"Hey, good lookin' out." Ralph nodded to the driver a few minutes later as the chauffeur pulled beside his black Riviera to let them out, then pressed the key fob and unlocked the door. "How you feel Young Homie?" He climbed behind the wheel as Timothy entered on the passenger's side.

"Crazy." Timothy glanced out the window with a tiny smirk on his face as he fastened his seatbelt.

"Welcome to the club, man." Ralph snickered. "Hey, it ain't over 'til it's over. I couldn't do this job if I hadn't earned my stripes in this here game called life. Trust me, I wasn't always straight-laced. I use my battle scars to help others... it helps to ease the pain in my own life. For the most part, anyway. Either way, all the pain will never completely go away but we just learn to bear it as we ask the Master to lead us according to His will. His plan for our lives. Like I said, I'm never judging because I've been through the storm. And that ain't no crack, that's a fact."

"First time I heard that one." Timothy leaned back in the seat. "Not bad for a older cat... I guess."

"Old school for life Young Buck." Ralph snorted. "Don't let the age fool ya, though. And most definitely don't let me hit the dance floor or I will wear you out boy, I got them moves." Ralph looked up at the sky and chuckled.

"Don't tell me - it's that crazy Jitter-Bug."

"On steroids, you ain't know?"

"If I didn't, I do now, unfortunately." Timothy shook his head in amusement. "You're crazy, you are aware of this, correct?"

"Hey, that's what keeps me sane, my man." Ralph pulled up in front of the Young Adult Risk program and parked as they headed inside to the receptionist's booth.

"What can I do for you today?" The secretary looked up from the computer.

"I was just wondering if I could speak with you in private for a minute?" Ralph motioned Timothy to have a seat as he stepped around the glass shield of the front desk and whispered to the employee. "Check it out, my man's a few years younger than our usual age requirement but he could still use a little supervision - at least until I can look into some other options... He definitely doesn't need to be alone right now, especially not out in these streets."

"Got it." The worker reached under the desk and pulled out some registration forms, then started the paperwork.

Chapter 8

"Are you sure you can handle the extra hours - you're already stretched to the limit and your work load is pretty heavy." Bryant's team manager inquired out of concern. "Not to mention you look extremely tired... I just don't want to see you work yourself into a frenzy."

"Thanks, I'm good though. Hey, anything for the wifey. You know she's got her eyes set on a new car and I wanna be able to give her what she wants. Nothing beats putting a smile on babe's face.

"Wow, must be nice. I only wish I knew love like that - she must really be some kind of special."

"Oh Brenda's a real doll - to say the least.."

"Evidently, but just out of curiosity - and it's probably none of my business, I only wished somebody loved me like that. Heck I'd take a 1970 Ford Pinto if someone gave it to me, but didn't you just buy her that brand spanking new silver BMW just last year?"

"Yeah, but now she's stuck on that Porsche Panamera."

"*Yikes*... she's got some pretty expensive taste."

"Awe yeah, my baby don't come cheap, that's for sure. But I don't mind 'cause she deserves it."

"Hey, you know what they say. Just ain't no tellin' what a satisfied woman might do... and I guess that goes for the man, too."

"You got that right... Happy wife - happy Life." Bryan poured the last of the asphalt onto the cracked pavement and laid the final row of bricks. It had been a long hard day, he let out a sigh of relief as he took off his construction gear and climbed into his old pickup truck as visions of a good home-cooked meal and his favorite sports team winning the playoffs danced in his head. Quickly shunning the idea of going to the local dive to hang out with the fellas to catch the game like he usually did, he started the engine and made a bee-line toward home to surprise the wife for a change. He smiled to himself as he stopped at the local vendor and picked out a dozen of long stem red roses, then headed home.

The house was unusually dark, he noticed as he peeled into the driveway and headed inside from the garage entrance. Then made his way up the stairs and tipped toward the back bedroom on the second level to investigate the faint sound of laughter. A shriek of boiling anger gushed through his veins as he peeked through the cracked door and lunged at his wife, shoving her across the room.

"DON'T!!!" She winced in pain as her back met the wall.

"This can't be my man Mike - how you gonna play me man, as far back as we go? I been knowing you since way back in the day, from cleaning the church after Sunday school to running the streets - you was my dawg!!!" Bryant grabbed him by the collar and squared up face to face.

"Don't hurt him!!!" Brenda shouted in horror as she leaped up from the floor and flung herself between the two men.

"Get out my way woman - you should've thought about that before you let this low down weasel into our bed!" He elbowed her away as he clenched his hands around Mike's neck as tight as he could.

"Hey man, slow down!" Mike choked on his words, grasping for air wrestling to free himself from the massive choke hold.

"Maybe you need to take your own advice for a change. You went behind my back!" Bryant continued to tighten his grip as Mike's eyes rolled to the back of his head.

"Baby please calm down..." Brenda pleaded frantically.

"How dare you..." He sneered angrily. "Don't you ever speak another word to me!"

"Baby please...."

"Yeah right, don't you baby me. And it's mighty funny you weren't saying that a minute ago when I first walked in here." Bryant tightened his grip as the veins bulged from Mike's temples pulsating in and out, oblivious to his wife's pleas. "Man, I thought you had my back. I gave you money when you got laid off from your job, worked on your car for free - I would've never in a million years played you like this.... Never!" Bryant strengthened his chokehold as Mike struggled to free himself.

"Hey, man... think about what you're doing..." Mike begged for his life as Brenda ran outside to summon help..

"He's out of control!!!" She screamed to the top of her lungs.

"What's going on???" Ralph looked up from the vacant lot and dropped the bag of cans, then instantly ran toward the house.

"My husband's inside fighting with someone and I'm afraid he's gonna choke him out - Please can you do something!" Brenda grabbed Ralph's hand and pulled him toward the house.

"You called the police?!"

"I can't find my phone, please help me!" She jumped up and down hysterically as she pulled him inside and ran to the back bedroom toward the two men wrestling on the floor as a crowd of neighbors gathered around the front stoop.

"Hey man - you don't wanna do this..." Ralph eased by the bed post and whispered.

"I caught him with my wife, man I will end him!" He shouted.

"I'm sorry, I know it hurts, this is a tough one. Trust me, I understand. But you don't want this on your track record. It's gonna ruin you." Ralph spoke calmly as he took a few steps closer.

"I work my tail of trying to provide for my wife - I even bought her a brand new luxury car and this is the thanks I get? And out of all the people she chooses to step out with - she chooses my best friend?! This was supposed to be one of my closest buddies. I knew him since I was knee-high to a grasshopper. We came up on the same side of the tracks, even went to the same church all the way up to adulthood. I knew him when he didn't have a pot to boil water in nor a window to throw it out of - and this dude tries to ruin my life like this?" He toughened his chokehold as Mike faded in and out, his eyes swollen into tiny little slits.

"Bryant please listen, you're gonna regret it, please..." Brenda whimpered frantically.

"Oh so now you're ready to reason things out?" He raged with anger.

"Hey, come on. I'm not saying it's easy..." Ralph intervened. "Look, you seem like a pretty level-headed guy. I can look around this home and see the hard work you've put into it, all the upgrades you've made. You can't just throw all that away. You worked too hard for this. Trust me, I can tell. I'm just trying to get you to think it out, man. Think about the years of hard work just swirling right down the drain, all because of one reckless decision. That's only gonna make matters worse for you, in the long run. Then you really won't have anything to show for your struggle - on top of the pain you're already dealing with... Be smart, man. Use your brain." He reasoned. "Come on, don't throw it all away."

"That's easy for you to say - put yourself in my shoes... I don't know what it is I want anymore." Bryant eased up his grip a little, then tightened back up.

"Hey, I'm not even saying you shouldn't be hurt. Who wouldn't be, you're human.. You have every right to feel betrayed but it takes two to tango and obviously there's some previous issues going on in the marriage that should have been addressed or none of you would be in this situation right now. Maybe over time, when things calm down, you can sort it all out. Who knows, maybe it might be best to go your own separate ways if it's gotten to this point. Don't look at it as a sign of weakness, take it as a sign of maturity and knowing when to let go... when to walk away. I don't believe in the impossible, but at this level of betrayal it will probably be extremely difficult to ever trust again in this marriage. It's definitely something to think about." Ralph reached out to massage his shoulder.

"I never even deserved this, man..." Bryant looked over at Brenda as the tears welled up in his eyes. "I was good to you. I gave you everything you could have ever wanted. You could have told me you weren't happy. You could have told me you wanted out." He wailed in agony as he released his grip on Mike's neck and stood up.

"Hey, you got this man... let it out... it's okay.." Ralph embraced him in a brotherly hug as a few neighbors filed inside followed by a sheriff.

"Hey officer - he got it. He's good." He assured the man in uniform as he helped Mike up.

"Thank God, nobody was hurt." A neighbor grabbed Brenda by the hand and led her into another room.

"You okay?" Ralph nodded to Mike as the officers escorted Bryant to the squad car.

"I guess I'll be aight." He rubbed the swollen bruises around his neck.

"Hey man, you might wanna go get checked out anyway... just to be sure." Ralph glanced at Brenda as she entered the room in a nervous wreck.

"I'm going to stay with family for a while." She packed a few items and left with the neighbor.

"Take care." Ralph watched her exit then followed Bryant out to his truck.

"I'm never one to judge - but you got off relatively easy that time although I wouldn't try that again if I were you. I've seen situations like this end up a whole lot worse. Especially considering how he had the upper hand over you back there."

"I'm not proud of what I did..." Mike hung his head in shame. "This is a real wake-up call..." He studied the ground in deep thought. "A wake-up call that it's time for a real change in my life."

"I sure do hope so... because next time, there might not be a next time." Ralph handed him his card and watched him pull off, then headed to his car.

*****

Ralph sat in his car lost in deep thought, trying to process it all. Make sense of everything as he fought to clear his mind. *What was the world coming to?* He pondered the question, his mind deeply distraught as he stared off into the distance. *Why did everybody seem to be so uptight and always on the defense?* It was as though destroying one another was the new trend. So much hostility and injustice. People always looking for flaws and a reason to judge the next man, instead of trying to find ways to help one another out.

Ralph stared out the window trying to gather his thoughts as he took in a breath of fresh air, inhaling the gentle breeze drifting from the peaceful pond, trying to calm his nerves for a moment. Then quickly hopped out and hit the walking trail to shake the negative emotions.

"Sorry to bother you sir, but can you happen to spare a few singles, please?" A feeble voice mumbled from behind with a sense of urgency.

"What's happening, son?" Ralph turned around and stopped in his tracks as he glanced at the narrow figure of the lonely looking young man walking with his head hung low, then waited for him to catch up. His tense expression drawn and lost in despair as he grumbled to himself.

"Not a whole lot, Just trying to cop a little change so I can put something on my stomach." He rubbed his belly as his ribcage buldged beneath the dingy T-shirt.

"How do you usually eat young man?"

"Most of the time I don't."

"How do you survive, I mean where is home?" Ralph froze in disbelief.

"The gutter."

"I'm sorry to hear that..."

"I guess it ain't bad as it could be, I suppose - seeing as though I'm the last survivor of my entire family." The young man looked away.

"That's a pretty tough situation."

"Tell me about it - between sickness, hard times and everything else in between, everybody's gone. I been out here in these streets practically my whole life trying survive."

"So what're you gonna do about it?"

"What can I do but roll with the punches."

"What you know about rollin' with the punches, you look mighty young to be going through all of this."

"Yeah, I am. I'm nineteen years young, matter fact." He looked up at the sky.

"I believe I can help you."

"I doubt it, but thanks for the concern."

"I'm pretty sure there's something I can do. I head the Young Adult At-Risk Program downtown." He reached out to shake the youngster's hand.

"Oh, that's right. I thought I remembered your face from somewhere around the way."

"Yes, you look slightly familiar too, but I've worked with so many people getting them signed up for outreach services and helping people in need that it's hard to keep track. But it's my mission - eventhough sometimes it seems like it backfires."

"I can believe it. That's why I don't really like to ask nobody for help because folks be trippin' and they start treating you funny, like you don't matter, just because you fell on hard times. So I just made up my mind I'd rather struggle on my own until I get on my feet."

"Well, you definitely don't have to worry about that with me - it's my calling and I love what I do. It's nothing more fulfilling than helping people in need, eventhough it often comes with its challenges. But in order to be helped you gotta want the help and all I keep hearing you say is how you keep refusing it because of what people may think."

"It's not that, I just don't want nobody feeling like they owe me nothin'. I don't want no handouts."

"But it's not about handouts. It's about being grateful and recognizing a blessing when you see one."

"Yeah, but in the streets it's hard to know who to trust. Plus, it seem like everytime I let my guard down somebody tries to cross me." The young man rubbed his temples in distress like he had weathered a thousand storms.

"Trust me, I often feel the exact same way but it's times like these when we must be strong and continue to brave on. Fight the good fight... Be encouraged."

"I guess..."

"Hey, you know what they say, our greatest tests can lead to our greatest testimonies." Ralph handed him his card.

"Thank you sir. You know, you really are encouraging me right about now." He slid it in his pocket and looked down at the ground.

"However I can help, son."

"A couple singles would be great. It'd really help me out a lot."

"Gotcha, let me see what I can do." Ralph pulled out his wallet and pulled out a wad of bills and handed him a twenty dollar bill. "That oughta tide you over until we get you into the work program down at the center. Come on, let's head on over there and get you a room so you can get off these streets for starters. And at least you have got a little change in your pocket, it's the best I can do for now."

"I sure do appreciate it, sir." He stuffed the money in his pocket. "But I'm willing to believe you can do just a little bit better than that." The young man plucked the entire stack of bills from his hand and ran off as Ralph flopped down on the park bench in defeat. He had done all he could to help everyone he could, yet all he seemed to get in return for his good deeds were people taking advantage, time and time again. *What was the point in even trying?* He thought to himself as he slumped forward trying to come to terms with what had just occurred.

Was there any good left in mankind at all? He questioned the reality of life as he felt his countenance slowly drifting away. What was the point of someone trying to hold on to their faith and always trying to do what is good, when evil was always present? "He weighed the troubles of the world on his shoulders. He had always tried to do what was right, even down to giving his very last and now someone had taken the last little bit he had. He rocked back and forth trying to calm his nerves. That was all of the money he had left from his aluminum can side hustle and now he didn't even have that. He thought about the money he had just donated to the local charity as he took out his wallet and pulled out the last ten dollar bill stored behind his license beneath the plastic flap. A crash of reality tortured his mind as it finally dawned on him that where he had seen the young man's face and that he was one of the juvenile delinquents he had helped in the At Risk Young Adult Program. Providing him a place to stay and keep him off the streets until they notified his parents.

How could someone, especially that young, be so cruel to mistreat someone who reached out and ignored their own needs all to help him get off the streets and offer him a safe place to stay in a program that provided everything for him in his worst time of need. Ralph's heart sunk into his shoes as he questioned his own sanity. What could have possibly made him so cruel at such a young age? Where was the justice... and what was the point of it all?

He wasn't looking for accolades or a kickback. He just wanted to bring some peace into the world. A catalyst to spark love and change within a society filled with so much pain. He thought long and hard about his calling and the sheer act of kindness, in itself. The power it carried to transform entire lives and promote healing in a hurting world.

Help mankind as a whole and generate a more compassionate society. It was the single component that constantly drove him to want to spread love and make a difference... And now the world had managed to take even that. He felt the anger rush up inside as the tears gushed down his face.

The sun's brilliance was slowly beginning to fade as he looked up into the sky and then headed for the main Boulevard. It had still been a beautiful day, despite of what had happened. He bargained with himself as a rowdy group of teenagers raced down the avenue on their skateboards, knocking him backwards as he tumbled to the ground. Still reeling from the sudden impact, he knew in his heart it was definitely time to take a break from it all. He staggered toward the corner store and leaned on the front door as he closed his eyes, struggling to maintain his balance.

"You can't loiter here sir, this is private property." The heavy voice boomed out of nowhere, startling him back to reality as he felt a sharp poke in his side from the hard object.

"Just trying to get myself together, give me a minute man." He looked up at the store owner.

"I get it, just do it somewhere else, that's all. Like I said, this here is private property. Now get moving."

"Hey, I just took a pretty bad fall earlier when those skateboarders almost crashed into me and I'm still trying to catch my balance. I think I must have sprung something – for real. I'm just trying to take it easy for a few minutes, if you don't mind. Believe me, I'm not trying to stay here I'm just trying to regain my balance. My hip still hurts but like I said, I'll be up in a second, I promise..."

"That has nothing to do with me - now be gone or I'm calling the police!" The store owner raged angrily and pointed toward the sidewalk. "It's plenty of room by the sewer now go! This is the back property of my business and I want you outta here now or else!! So you can go on your own or be escorted. Either way is fine with me as long as I don't see you anymore."

"Look, save your energy man. I just told you I had an accident and you can't even help me out? Come on, you know who I am and you know I got a car. You see me around this area helping people out ever day of the week. I'm only parked a few blocks up the street." Ralph pulled himself together and slowly wobbled back to his automobile and climbed inside, suddenly noticing the broken glove compartment door as he quickly searched through his paperwork in disbelief. Then immediately pulled out his cell phone and began dialing as an explosion of pain in his lower back traveled down his leg.

"Hey, what's happening?" The assistant manager's husky voice appeared on the other end of the line.

"Check this out Chuck man, I'm gonna really need for you to take the wheel for a minute and run things... I need to step away for a minute..." Ralph hesitated.

"What's up, I was wondering where you been. I've been trying to reach you for I don't know how long, where you at?"

"I'm good - I just need to take break, get my head right. It's a little too much goin' on right about now. Hey, I'll explain it all to you later - you got me or what?"

"Look here partner, take all the time you need, I got you. Just hit me up if anything comes up and keep me posted."

"Will do, thanks Bro." Ralph disconnected the call and hopped on the expressway as he headed toward the country to clear his mind before it all went bad and he really lost touch.

Chapter 9

Vicky stumbled down the dark avenue and cut through the alley. The streets were pitch black but she knew she had to keep going, in spite of the vicious hunger pains racking her empty stomach. She lifted the top of the garbage barrel and peeked inside, searching for something to eat as a piece of rye bread caught her attention.

Quickly picking through the rubble, she dug out the tattered bun and examined both sides closely, then stuck it in her mouth. Her head was still reeling as she felt herself growing dizzier and dizzier, desperately craving for water. The pain in her neck growing more intense as she crouched down between the two trash containers and sat on the ground. Everyone had written her off. Tossed her out just like the trash in the barrels, she fought back the sting of tears welling up in her eyes, refusing to give in to her emotions.

There was no place to go... no place to hide from her nemesis. The shelter was just too dangerous and now Carlotta had managed to slip her way through the cracks of the Adult Risk Program. Vicky consoled herself as she looked around the dark alleyway, searching her pockets for the tiny flip phone Miss Genevieve had given her. She could still hear movement but had no idea where it was coming from as a tall looming figure suddenly appeared in her peripherals.

"Who are you?" She attempted to summon her strength, involuntarily surrendering beneath his massive strength, she fought back with all her might as she felt herself slipping further and further into darkness.

*****

Several hours had passed as Vicky sat forward and slowly came to. Cold drizzles of rain pelted down on her bare skin as she adjusting her clothing and hopped to her feet, then headed back down the dark alley. The sidewalk was a blur as she trudged toward the boulevard and headed back to the shelter. Life had taken all that was left... drained her of what little integrity and self respect she had. She fought back the humiliation and shame as she pulled the tattered jacket closed, bracing against the cold rain she fled toward the Salvation Army entrance.

"How may we help you, today?" The desk clerk looked up in bewilderment as she took in Vicky's broken image. "What happened to you, are you okay?" She dropped her pen in shock and rushed from behind the desk.

"I can't do this anymore... I need to sign myself back in." Vicky felt herself about to collapse as the receptionist helped her up into a chair.

"I remember you, where've you been all this time?" She summoned the guard then ran to find a nurse.

"I just left for..." Vicky's voice trailed off as she broke down in tears.

"Just try to relax now." The staff nurse rushed into the room with a cool compress. "She's been here before, although I can't remember the exact date she left. But I *do* remember her." She grabbed an alcohol wipe and directed her toward the back room. "Don't you remember me?"

"I'm tired." Vicky murmured as the sound of the nurse's voice dipped in and out in a blur. "Just want to lay down." She placed her hands on her head trying to ease the lightheadedness.

"Yes, but first we need to make sure you're okay. Are you in any pain - do you need to go to the hospital? Who did this to you?"

"Please, I just want everything to go away." Vicky sobbed, bobbing back and forth in the chair.

"Come with me." The nurse escorted her to the back office and stuck a thermometer in her mouth. "Temperature's fine." She read the numbers on the glass gadget and removed the plastic hygiene cover and discarded it.

"Now can I go and lay down?" Vicky rolled off the table and curled up on the floor as the tall wheatish complexioned doctor entered the room and helped her up.

"I'm Dr. Ross, what seems to be going on?" He flashed the medical penlight into her pupils as he examined her eyes.

"She doesn't seem to be too coherent." The nurse placed the ice pack on the table and stepped out of the way.

"Seems to be some type of trauma." He placed the stethescope onto her chest and listened to her heartbeat as he checked the charts. "Vitals are fine." He paused for a second, a look of concern etching across his face. "Did someone hurt you? You can trust me." He placed his arm around her shoulder.

"No, I just want to sleep." She pleaded.

"She was just in here less than two weeks ago." The nurse swabbed Vicky's forehead with a fresh alcohol wipe.

"Can someone please sign her back in?" Doctor Ross looked at the receptionist with serious concern.

"Definitely." She answered immediately and rushed off to start the paperwork.

*****

Why did everything have to be so dad-blasted hard and confusing all of the time. Vicky pondered, lost in deep thought. *And why did the bad guys always seem to win in life, what was really goin' on?* She questioned the conundrums of life as she stepped out of the shower at the shelter and toweled off, then slipped into a pair of fresh scrubs the Salvation had provided for free as she contemplated the harsh reality of her existence. She stiffened her reserve as the soreness in the side of her head slammed as a painful reminder of life on the streets as she exited the bathroom and started toward her room.

The thought of reaching back out to Ralph just to touch base crossed her mind as she realized she had lost the card with all of his contact information. The options were becoming more and more dismal and useless as she tried to sort them out, fighting the urge to just give up on the whole thing. And life in itself. She knew he had done everything he knew to do, everything in his power to help. The Young

Adult Program seemed to be the perfect opportunity and solution at first, *but what could help a loser?* She diminished her own self worth. She could feel herself will drift further and further away as she considered going back.

But there was no one there to protect her from the vultures, especially Carlotta - who was queen of the heathens. She knew the streets like she knew the back of her hand, Vicky rationalized, staring out of the window. It was time to make a move but in which direction? She contemplated. The best thing to do was to stay out of the way, stay on guard and stay smart. Lay low just in case she had to fight off the wolves and fend for herself... by fair means or foul.

Life was not a game and never had been. But now it was real. *Really* real. The dizzying headache blurred her sight as she headed toward the bathroom and looked into the mirror, then pulled her hair into a ponytail. The world had taken everything else but she refused to let the enemy win. She needed a break. Catch a breath of fresh air and clear her head, she lifted the window and climbed out, inhaling the cool air as she walked toward the major boulevard where all the action took place.

The streets were filled with the usual afternoon traffic as people milled about taking care of business or on their usual lunch break as she browsed past the small businesses and shops and relaxed. It was way too many people out for Carlotta to rear her ugly head, at least in broad daylight. She only struck in the dark where she thought she could hide, just like the coward she truly was. Vicky assured herself as she rested her eyes on the "Hiring" sign posted on the newly built cafe then opened the door and stepped inside.

"Greetings." The jovial woman in bifocals smiled from behind the counter.

"Hello." Vicky felt the warmth as she glanced at the delicate antique figurines incased in wooden cabinets, adding to the cozy ambiance of the quaint little shop. "This is new, right?" Vicky slipped off her jacket and slid onto a barstool.

"Yes ma'am...*Brand Spanking*." The woman grabbed the brewing pot of hot coffee and poured it into a porcelain cup then slid it across the counter. "Help yourself." She beamed.

"Don't mind if I do." Vicky welcomed the kind gesture as she blew off the steam and took a careful sip. "Beautiful decor." She looked around the freshly designed cafe decked in bright yellow bar stools lined against the dark oak bar and a few dining tables scattered about.

"Thanks, yes I have to admit it does have a very nice feel to it... kind of soothing." She complied in agreement. "So what brings you in today? Just out and about catching a little me-time, I suppose."

"Most definitely."

"Well I heard that. Hey sometimes you just gotta do what you gotta do in order to stay sane, ya know?"

"Exactly." Vicky quickly glanced at the waitresse's name tag then out of the large cafe windows into the glistening sunlight.

"Sorry, don't mean to be rude, I'm Audrey." The woman tugged at her hair net and pushed up her bifocals.

"Nice to meet you, I'm Vicky... Just out trying to clear my mind, I guess." She reached for a packet of sugar as she fought back the tears.

"I *do* understand, feel free to let it all out. Go on ahead and vent. Trust me, this here is the safety zone. Been down a time or two myself, so I can definitely relate."

"Thanks for the encouragement... I'm just trying to get back up on my feet. Just feeling like I've been down too long. It's crazy. *For real-for real.*" Vicky took another sip of coffee to calm her nerves.

"Oh I'm already knowing...and it's definitely not a nice feeling, either. You feel like the whole *world* is against you. Been there - done that. Only the strong survive, but just remember one thing - don't nothing last forever. And I do mean *nothing*. You know what they say, hard times don't last always. Get knocked down ten times get up twenty. That's the way you have to be in this life."

"I'm so sick and tired of struggling, though. I mean, when is it ever going to end? Sometimes I just feel like giving up." Vicky hung her head and weeped. "For some reason I just can never seem to catch a break in this life."

"You're gonna be alright sis, just don't you worry." Audrey pulled a tissue from the box and handed it to her. "You know working this here cafe job, I hear so many stories from folks down on life who feel the exact same way. But I always try to encourage people. If you just don't give up and you can suffer through the hard times, one day you're going to reap a pay day for all your struggles. Believe it when I tell you. You just hang on in there, queen.

I would hate to see you give up right before your breakthrough. Who knows, it might be right around the corner. Do you know how many folks have given up on that ninety-eighth try? And their win was just around that ninety-ninth corner... if only they had of just stuck it out. Seriously though, it's something to think about."

"You're right." Vicky dried her eyes. "I guess I'm just sick and tired of being sick and tired, is all I'm saying."

"I get it. And I know life can be tough and not to sound like a cliche`, but good things really do come to those who wait. You just seem like such a nice genuine person - with a good heart. I want to see good come your way for a change."

"Thank you Audrey. I try not to let this crazy world get me down. And thanks for all the kind words, it's rare nowadays. And much appreciated." Vicky guzzled down the last drop of her coffee with a sense of renewal as she listened to Audrey's pep talk. It had been eons since anyone had even thought about supporting her. It was as though everyone wanted to see her fail...succumb to her circumstances, she glanced at the hiring sign in the window. "Need some help?"

"So glad you asked, yes ma'am we certainly do." Audrey snickered. "Are you kidding me or what? It's a little slow around this time of day, but in the evening? Girl bye." Audrey rolled her eyes and shook her head. "And that's the truth and I'm sticking with it." She slapped the counter and howled with laughter.

"Really?" Vicky sighed in relief.

"Definitely, matter of fact you seem like the perfect person for the job - there should be no problem getting you in."

"Seriously?"

"I don't see why not." Audrey reached into a drawer and pulled out the one page application and slid it across the counter with an ink pen.

"You should give it a try. Hey, you never know."

"Wow, you make me feel like a brand new person, this must really be my day." Vicky hesitated for a moment. "The Salvatation of Army shelter is my only place of residence at this moment so I'll have to use that as my current address. I truly hope that doesn't mess up my chances."

"Honey please, with that winning attitude of gratitude you've got the world at your feet. You just don't know, that's exactly what we need around here. You seem to be in it to win it, as they say. You'd be amazed how that could brighten up some of our customer's day. And like I said before, in here is a non-judgement zone and because you're so awesome, I'm gonna try and sneak in a good word to the manager, how's that?" Audrey placed her hands on her hips and winked.

"Wow, I don't even know what to say, I guess I'm speechless. Thank you." Vicky overflowed with excitement.

"No worries and you don't have to say a thing - your smile is worth a thousand words." Audrey chuckled.

"I don't think I have the main phone number at the shelter..." Vicky zoomed through the application as quickly as possible, then paused for a second.

"Don't even worry about it, I can look it up. Plus, I know a few people over there anyways. Somebody will touch base and let you know if the manager decides to drop a line ... Don't worry we'll take good care of ya."

"God bless you Audrey." Vicky handed her the application and walked toward the exit.

"You too, sis. And you have yourself a wonderful rest of your day." Audrey smiled as Vicky disappeared out the door, then placed the job application between her fingers and ripped it to shreds then tossed it in the garbage.

*****

Vicky knew it was only a matter of time before Carlotta would catch back up to her. The clock was ticking and the streets were listening. She had to act fast." She thought to herself, strategizing in silence as she cleaned up the tiny area she had been re-assigned at the shelter, then headed down to the kitchen. In her heart of hearts, she knew it was going to be a fight, but she had to get out of there, eventhough the staff doctor had pulled some strings to get her back in and off the streets out of danger. She took a deep breath, overcome by the urge to faint as the pit of her stomach churned from weeks of starvation.

Carefully tipping, she braced against the wall for support and eased out into the hallway, then headed for the locked cafeteria doors. "Please Don't Lock It..." She ran toward the service window and banged on the plexiglass with all of her might.

"Sorry, we close at five." The cafeterian nonchalantly slipped the padlock onto the metal fixture of the rim of the window and turned her back.

"Come on, please. It's just a few minutes after. Don't you remember me? Ma'am please don't be that way I'm starving." Vicky pleaded as she watched the woman shut off the lights and walk out the door. "Will

Somebody Please Listen To Me!" Vicky clamored for attention as she ran down the hall, collapsing amid a sea of gaping stares and whispers as a staff member ran out into the hall and helped her up. Then led her to the nurse's station in the back room.

"Chin up." The nurse rubbed her forehead with a damp cloth. "You're going to be just fine - you've been through so much, dear." She smiled gently then handed her a boxed lunch with a juice. "Something to take the edge off... help you sleep." She dropped a tiny blue pill in the small plastic cup and placed it on the nightstand. "But you gotta promise to finish all of your food and drink this entire juice first, so you don't get nauseated in order for it to work right, okay sweetie?" She watched as Vicky surveyed the little round capsule and popped it in her mouth, then gulped down the juice and opened the box of food.

Chapter 10

It had been an entire year since Ralph had left the scene and the torment he had endured had pressured him to the point of giving up on life. He sat for a few minutes taking it all in, then got out of his car and walked toward the Boulevard. Nothing had changed... He surveyed the place he hadn't seen in years. The local dives and restaurants all looked the same as he walked past a group of street heads sharing a bottle as he continued to explore the strip. Then headed back to the old post office to relax on the brick staircase for a minute and collect his thoughts.

The bad always seemed to come out on top and the good always seemed to get left behind, so what was the use of even trying to do what was right - where was the justice? He wondered to himself for the umpteenth time as he leaned back on the steps of the old weathered building and looked across the street, then reached in his pocket and grabbed a fist full of coins and tossed them up in the air as they scattered along the Boulevard. It was all a lie anyway... he felt his fortitude waning as he pulled out the bottle of painkillers and examined the overdose warning, wondering what the after life would be like. He read the label over and over contemplating if it was worth it all.

He had spent his entire life reaching out trying to help others, but who would miss him when he was gone? No one. He negotiated back and forth in his mind. He'd lived his entire life being the invisible man and no one cared about a loser because everything he touched turned to crap. He unscrewed the bottle and surveyed the cluster of capsules.

"Hey, stranger." He heard the familiar voice call from behind and quickly turned around frozen in shock as Timothy's crispy clean cut physique appeared out of nowhere.

"My man, I didn't even recognize you - you look...."

"Quite dapper?" Timothy chuckled sarcastically as he smoothed the neatly trimmed moustache that complimented his fresh fade.

"To put it mildly." Ralph took a few steps backwards to check out his fresh digs. "Hey, you really clean up well you know?"

"Thanks man... I do my best." He joked spinning around, his young muscular frame decked in an expensive sports jersey and designer jeans and kicks.

"I see you've been hitting the gym lately - you're looking strong and healthy these days." Ralph gripped Timothy's hand in a fist shake and bumped shoulders. "Life's been good to you, I see."

"Yeah, they keeping me on my toes over there where I work, I guess."

"And where exactly is this place, I might need to look into getting myself signed up. Maybe I can get back to how I used to be... but I ain't speakin' on much..." Ralph joked.

"I hear ya... It's the brand new youth facility downtown."

"The Boy's Home for juvenile's division where I dropped you off?"

"Yes sir. I'm district manager, basically over the entire region although I spend a lot of my time at this particular location mentoring the youth. Support services, counseling, helping them get jobs and transitioning them back into society... whatever it is they need."

"I'm proud of you, son. You really made my day - I've been walking around here moping all day long and you know that's not even me but it's been kind of a rough time here lately. Life has a way of making you feel like giving up sometimes, especially when you try to do good and it seems like nothing ever comes of it."

"Please don't ever feel that way, we need people like you. People like you make a difference, especially with this younger generation out here today. They're faced with so much more than the previous and they need someone who genuinely cares to show them the way."

"Wow, you really got my head in a whirl, son. You seem so different now. So mature and evened out, what happened to change you like this?"

"It was God... and you. Had it not been for you taking the first step and making the effort to help get me off these streets it ain't no telling where I would be right about now in my life. Probably strung out or locked up at the rate I was going, who knows. But you changed all that for me. You changed my life. You showed me a better way. You taught me how to be strong. But most of all... you *believed* in me." Timothy led the way as they walked to the Salvation Army center and went inside, then headed upstairs past the juvenile division towards the elaborate back office overlooking downtown.

"So this is you?" Ralph looked around the expansive office embellished with a fancy cherry oak desk and furnishings as Timothy smiled ecstatically and shook his head. "Man, this is marvelous."

"Thanks, yeah I ended up in the all boy's home after I finally got out of detention and it was the best thing that ever happened to me. I mean, it was definitely a rough start but I just hung in there. Then one day I realized that if I wanted things to ever change in my life I had to put in the work because nobody was coming to rescue me. Nobody was coming to save the day... so I had to man-up. But had it not been for you initiating the whole process, taking me under your wing and getting me signed into the program, I would still be out here hustling and trying to get over on people."

"My heart is bursting with joy for you, son. You have no idea how it feels to hear you talk that way - I always knew you had it in you."

"Hey thanks for everything, Ralph... and most of all for believing in me, man... You showed me tough love. You showed me what it really means to be a man and take ownership and responsibility. You showed me that someone really did care what happens to me. You saved my life, man... and I could never repay you. I look at these young cats out here today and all they need is some guidance... some direction."

"You made my day man, that's all I can say..." Ralph fought back the tears overwhelmed with compassion as he looked at the new man Timothy had become, listening to his heartfelt testimony. "I had no idea I made such a huge impact. I agree, you'd be surprised what just a simple kind word or gesture can do for someone's entire life perspective. People are out here going through some crazy stuff. These are crazy times we're living in." Ralph summarized.

"That part I do recognize - but the way things are nowadays and attitudes, it's almost taboo to reach out to people." Timothy countered.

"And why do you think that is?"

"I guess people just aren't friendly anymore, like your generation was. The world changed. It's grown colder and most people seem so angry and like they don't even care or wanna be bothered most of the time." Timothy looked despondent, his eyes slightly downcast as he looked off in the distance.

"Yeah but don't believe the hype, youngster. Sometimes it's the exact opposite and all that is - is a front. A lot of people try to mask their true feelings and hide their pain... hide what they're going through, but deep down inside they're miserable, secretly dying inside. Silently crying out for help, but just don't know how to say it. Some people may even be trapped in desperate situations that they're either too prideful to face reality or fearful of looking vulnerable, so they act cool but deep inside they're really not. They're playing hard just to save face." Ralph spoke words of wisdom.

"That's a lot to take in but I appreciate your life lessons sir and I one hundred percent agree. It's definitely not a simple task when it comes to evaluating somone's character or what they will and won't do because there's so many masks in the streets and in the world. So it can be a hard thing to detect. Especially when you're not from the streets and you don't really understand that life. But many times, those are the main ones going through the most. They just know how to play it off, who to confide in and who not to, because it's possible to confide in the wrong person. Or even your enemy. So we must be careful in this life... we must know how to move, when to speak and when to be silent."

"You have grown light years, youngster. It's like talking to a whole new Timothy in comparison to the previous one."

"That I am. Hey, the streets taught me alot, most of all to be careful. Especially because you never know what type of issues or problems people are dealing with and a lot of times those are the same things that drive them into the life they're living. For some, it's the only way out. So keep encouraging people man, because for some, it's the only light they will ever see in this world. I'm saying, I really appreciate you yo'. You could have looked down your nose at me like everybody else did, but you didn't do that. You didn't write me off like all the other doubters. Instead, you knew the real me despite what it looked like from the outside and gave me a chance. But why?" Timothy looked up in confusion.

"That's just the way I'm wired, Timothy. Everyone goes through situations and circumstances in life - so who are we to judge one another? While one man celebrates a victory, somewhere else another man suffers a loss and you never know who could be next... it could be you or me. No man stays winning forever, just like no man stays down forever. Their are seasons in this life, although some may last longer than others."

"All I know is that's the way everybody has treated me ever since I been on this earth, so I can relate to the rebels of the younger generation. All my life I've been an outcast. Never have blended in anywhere. That's why I started doing whatever I very well pleased, how I wanted and when I wanted. I mean why not? I stopped caring about the next man because the next man never cared about me."

"I understand how you feel but that still doesn't make it right." Ralph interjected.

"Never said it did, I'm just explaining what drove me in the direction I was headed in and some folks never understand what causes so many to go left in life - it's like the entire world is clueless." Timothy shook his head.

"But the new you recognizes that you can't allow the actions of others to lead you down the wrong path in your own life.... and sometimes when you're a misfit and you don't blend in, there's a reason for it. A blessing and a gift inside of you or a calling up ahead in the future that you may not even be aware of. Oftentimes, that gift can feel like a heavy burden because everybody won't understand it or like the way it shines. Everyone won't always like the way you shine. And it's not about money or clout, it's about an inner wisdom, a glow of favor from above." Ralph analyzed.

"Without a doubt. I just know how it feels when everytime you try to stay on the right path, someone always comes along to throw you off. But like I always tell my mentorees, no one can throw you off your game unless you give them permission. And as difficult as it may seem, sometimes you just have to press beyond the negativity to get to the destination uniquely designed for you. I had to learn that the hard way and at a young age. You just can't allow anyone other than God to control you or you will never have any peace in life. Some of the youngsters I work with always come back with the question, "Am I supposed to just sit up here and let somebody run all over me and treat me any old kind of way then? And I always tell 'em, it's okay to stand up for yourself just try not to let it be in negative way."

"What a wise young man you've become."

"Hey thanks, all credit due to God almighty because one day I took a look in the mirror and I didn't like what I saw. I was on a path of destruction and I didn't want to be that person anymore. Being hateful, not caring about who I hurt and living any old kind of way just didn't appeal to me anymore... it just no longer served me and the day I ran into you and I was standing on the ledge of that rooftop about to end it all, I knew in my heart it was the last day I had planned to be on this here earth."

"Well I'm glad you're still here. You are wise beyond your years, son."

"Thanks for acknowledging my hard-won progress and it's definitely a blessing to still be here, eventhough it took everything inside of me to turn it all around. Trust me when I say, it truly didn't come over night. But the hiccups and struggles grew me into the man I am today. I used to feel so worthless in that place and it felt like I was just sinking lower and lower, like I would never get out. Even on the days when I was minding my own business homies was still trying to provoke me to do wrong, until one day I just surrendered my life to God and I turned it all over to Him.

Then some days, when things really got tough, I would get out my bible out and start looking up scriptures according to the issues I was dealing with at that time in my life. Then, next thing you know, one

Sunday morning the program directors took us to church and after that I started going on my own. That's when I noticed a change in my life. Like a whole new shift. Things started not to seem so bad after all and I started looking at stuff differently... that's when I realized I wanted a better life. So I started putting in the work, applying for jobs and staying out of trouble. Then eventually somebody opened a door for me and when I looked up and here I am..."

"Keep up the good work and the good fight." Ralph gave him another fist pump.

"I most definitely had to because there's nothing in the streets for me but ruin. My faith and struggles taught me to curb my temper and not let things get under my skin like I used to and feed my faith, instead. It helped me to develop patience and taught me a different perspective and the invaluable lesson that when people mistreat me for no reason at all not to take it personal because it's not about me. It's their issue to come to terms with and they have something on the inside that needs to be cleaned out. So they need to figure it out, it's their issue - not mine." Timothy dropped some final pebbles of spiritual wisdom.

"Youngster, that was a complete mouthful. You would be surprised just how long it takes some of us to finally figure that out - some an entire lifetime."

"Good seeing you, Bro." Timothy gave Ralph a brotherly hug. "Now I gotta get back to work before they give me an entire mouthful and fire me." He joked candidly. "I just wanted to give you your props. Hey, stop by and check me out anytime."

"Most definitely, stay up." Ralph shook his hand and watched in inspiration as Timothy headed back to his office.

Chapter 11

"It goes against the Second Amendment." Ralph stood next to the young man while the district attorney pleaded her client's case, her svelte figure and good looks baring a slightly resemblance of someone he had met in his past. He soaked in her attractive appearance as she slowly strutted her way back to her seat with an air of dignity.

"Does she stand a chance?" He leaned in and whispered.

"Well, she has the right to defend herself and her testimony of self defense is a definite credit on the side of her client, but I wouldn't get too excited if I were you. This judge has been known to overturn cases like these so it could still swing in the opposite direction and he could wind up ruling against it. I mean afterall, this isn't her first time. It could also end up in a locked jury and go into another trial or a possible plea of temporary insanity - which could either work for or against her, depending on how the lawyers argue the case."

"So which way do you think it's gonna lean... from a legal perspective.

"Case dismissed." The judge slammed the gavel against the wooden sound block.

"She should be locked up!" A voice screamed out randomly from the back of the room as a frail figure darted toward the front of the courtroom.

"Please Miss..." Ralph rushed in to intervene.

"I'm sorry, but this is a court matter." The sherriff quickly apprehended the fragile woman.

"All I need is a moment of your time.. Can I pray for her?" Ralph dashed over to the frail woman as she tumbled to the floor and placed her hands on her forehead in resignation.

"We need a medic." The uniformed officer spoke non-challantly into his radio as they waited for an ambulance to arrive.

"Are you okay?" The counselor's voice jarred Ralph back to reality.

"I feel for her..." He fought back the tears as he watched the marshalls escort the poor woman away.

"I definitely understand... and trust me, this process is never an easy thing to witness. We see all sorts of cases. Let's face it, it's heartbreaking to watch someone go through something like this."

"I just don't know how you do it." Ralph watched them load the poor woman onto the stretcher and pull off with yet another tortured soul inside.

"Like I said, it's never easy... hey, how about we take a quick little breather. I could really stand a good cup of coffee right now, how about you?"

"Best idea I've heard all day." Ralph followed her outside as they walked across the way to the local diner.

"Now I remember where I met you - you've definitely come a long way, you know that?"

"Thanks, I've always had a penchant for justice so I decided to enroll into an apprenticeship program over at the University, which will ultimately lead me on the path of finally earning my judicial degree. It's gonna take some time, but I'm here for it. I mean, what have I got to lose I'm in it to win it right?"

"Right." Ralph grinned in admiration.

"But most of all, I want to to give thanks to you from the bottom of my heart for inspiring me... for believing in me and looking out for me. It's been quite a journey, I'll tell you that much. When you found me out in the streets, that was one of the lowest points in my life. And I honestly believed I would have died had you not been there to save me." She looked him in his eyes as an endless trail of tears rolled down her face. "Thank you for saving my life."

"I'm honored..." Ralph pulled her into his chest and hugged her tight.

"Not a day goes by that I'm not haunted by the agony of his abuse and reminded of what he did to me. ... He took everything I had. My peace. My hope. And my self worth. For so long I felt hopeless, useless and empty. Trapped inside of a body that was no longer mine. Trapped inside a life that I was never meant to live. I wanted to get out but I just didn't know how. But that pain, the abuse and the trauma, made me the woman I am today. Had it not been for what I been through, I couldn't relate to my clients the way that I do so cases like these are automatically pro bono. That woman did what she had to do. She had no choice but to defend herself, plus she has no support."

Ralph stood in admiration as he compared the stark contrast of the once bewildered woman to the strong inspiration she had become, then spoke. "The only true defense we have in this life is the assurance of God. He is the one and only true defender of justice and He sees all, even in tough situations like these. He is the precise balancing scale of true virtue and integrity. He not only weighs the action, but also the intent. His power is infinite but we must also be mindful of who we permit in our lives. The spirits we connect to or allow to connect to us have a direct impact on the events of our life because just like there are spirits of light - there are also spirits of darkness as we both know.

There is good and there is evil and once you allow that wickedness to get inside, it can convert you right into darkness. It is easier to be converted into darkness than it is to be pulled into righteousness. Helping others the way you do is a wonderful gift of the spirit, but you must still keep a watchful eye not to allow too much of yourself to be compromised. It can happen even in the most obscure ways when you least expect it and before you know it, you've morphed into someone you no longer recognize." Ralph held the door then followed her inside the cafe.

"This is exactly what happened to me in that relationship. When I looked in the mirror, it was like someone else was staring back at me... It was terrifying."

Ralph reached for her hand as the woman broke down in tears. "It was an unhealthy soul tie but you always have signs. He won't lead you astray or allow you to enter into a force of darkness without warning, but oftentimes we tend to ignore our instincts and that subliminal whisper in the back of our mind. The tiny still voice we keep shrugging off. It's usually a subtle inkling that keeps nagging at us and just won't go away.

Then by the time we do take heed, it's more than likely too late and before we realize it we're in way over our heads and we find ourselves sinking deeper and deeper into quicksand. Things just keep getting worse and we end up feeling like there's no way out. But it is... There's always a way out. It may not be the popular route or our first choice and may even be the desolate one. The road less traveled or the route no one else wants to take." Ralph smiled and nodded at the waitress as she filled the tiny porcelain cups with piping hot coffee.

"But why?" The fragile woman peered out the window in a state of confusion.

"There's a multitude of reasons from different sides of the spectrum... Sacrifice, Pride... Fear. In order to follow that voice... the inclination has to come from within. It has already been pre-installed and instilled in us but we must first die to self. Our earthly beliefs and worldly desires. We must die to our own will. We don't have all the answers in this life and we must face the fact that we are not in control. We are not our own, nor can we do it on our own. We were created to depend on the Higher Power of our Creator and trying to figure it out on our own is a recipe for sheer disaster."

"I understand - but not fully."

"And that's quite alright, we're not supposed to understand everything. This is where we make some of our biggest mistakes. We weren't designed to figure this thing out and how could we? We don't have the capacity, the understanding or depth. There are too many wonders in the universe and the world around us, what lies beyond the sky and in heaven to ever fully comprehend. It's too vast for our understanding. There are innumerous things we will never fully conceive, nor were we meant to. Yet, we are all still created with a gift inside... a purpose. And you use yours very well, may I add. "

"I could never thank you enough sir, for all you've done for me and saving my life." Overwhelmed with gratitude, the counselor grabbed his hand and held it tight.

"Pleasure is all mine, keep the faith." Ralph smiled and headed toward the exit.

*****

"I had to give up my babies, remember me?" The homeless woman rocked back and forth. Ralph could see the heartache in her eyes as she passed him by. She was back out on the streets. Everyday he watched her pacing. Circling the block, fading deeper and deeper into an abyss of obscurity. And everyday no one did anything to help her. It was as if she didn't matter, her pain and her life, insignificant... Ralph stood off to the side as he watched her pause for a moment barefooted, as she paced the hard surface of the concrete sidewalk. Oblivious to the bitter cold as she gazed through the cluster of dining tables, patrons and undesirable glares.

"How could I forget..." Ralph quickly stuffed the cans into a plastic bag and tied it in a knot then looked up in dismay. "I thought you would still be at the shelter after I got you all signed up - what happened?"

"Well, I signed myself back out. You know everything I owned is gone, the storm took it all away. Home, furniture, clothes, what little change we did have, all of it's underwater, swept away. Why should my babies suffer though, right? I'll happily sleep on the streets any day of the week. Long as they're good, safe and sound, that's all that matters. Nobody wanted to help us, anyhow. I asked for some but everybody just turned their backs on us. Stepped right on over us like we was trash in the streets. Guess they just didn't wanna be bothered." She broke down in tears. "I'm sick and tired of this life."

"Who is they?" Ralph's heart dropped as he cleared the lump in his throat, then spoke.

"The people at the place. Everybody really. I shouldn't even be going through this in the first place. Those are the same folks who promised to help us. They were supposed to renovate our home through that state grant program and just dropped the ball on us. Them and all the people I called that hung up on me, including all the folks in the streets who stepped over us like we were animals. Everybody failed us, all parties involved. So I had no choice. I had to do what was best for my family and see that my children were taken care of until I can get back up on my feet."

"Did you reach out to anyone for emergency support services?" Ralph took off his jacket and placed it over her shoulders.

"I did and when I went back to Social Services they closed the door in my face. Then I went to the housing authority to fill out an application and they ripped it up in my face, told me not to come back until my name gets pulled off the waiting list."

"And did they have any idea how long that might take?" He listened carefully as she snuggled beneath his cloak.

"Who knows, they never said..."

"So you're literally just hanging around in the streets waiting for a call?"

"Yes sir, but the catch is, I don't even have a phone. It was a part of my lost belongings so I just try to keep going back over there to check on things, whenever I get a chance."

"What is your means of transportation?"

"Walking." She looked down at her bare feet. "I have no money and definitely no car to get around in."

"What about public assistance?"

"But I need an address in order to get it started."

"This is crazy..." Ralph shook his head in exasperation.

"I know, and they won't even let me see my babies. Everytime I go over there they just get up and lock the door on me like I'm some stranger off the streets. They know I miss my babies and they won't even let me in..." She sobbed uncontrollably.

"Take me to your children." Ralph pulled her into his arms and led her to his car.

"I can't take it anymore, this pain is destroying me." She climbed into the front passenger's seat and placed her head on the dashboard for a moment, then buckled her seatbelt.

"Point me in the direction." He weaved through traffic. "I know it seems impossible, but you gotta stay strong if you want things to turn around. You can't give up now, you've gotta roll up your sleeves and fight."

"Everything is against me. It's like everybody wants to see us down and I don't know why. All the people I went to for help just kicked us at our lowest moment. Kicked us when we was down." She signaled as he made a right turn at the next corner."

"There isn't anyone you could call on - no family or friends?"

"No one..." She stared helplessly out the window and pointed to the white building on the left side of the street."

"Well all that's about to change." Ralph pulled up in front of the orphanage and parked. "You okay?"

"I'm just shook up right now." She paused, struggling to gain her composure.

"I got it - it's okay... By the way, I don't think I caught your name - I'm Ralph... and you are?"

"I'm Roxanne and I could never repay you."

"Hey don't worry about it, I'm happy to help." He hopped out and went around to the passenger side and opened the door. "Come on, pull yourself together and let's do this. I got your back." He straightened up the collar of her flimsy cotton shirt then headed inside toward the front desk. "May I please borrow a moment of your time, if that's not too much to ask?" Ralph spoke gently as the clerk looked up from the desk and rolled her eyes.

"All depends... what do you need assistance with?"

"I really need to speak with a social worker, if that's at all possible."

"You need to make an appointment, we're not accepting walk-ins currently." She glanced over at Roxanne's tattered clothing and quickly looked away.

"You know I come in here almost every single day and you keep turning me away. You know who I am. I just want to see my babies." The words sputtered from her mouth, her heart overflowing with anguish.

"Relax, I got this..." Ralph reached in his pocket and pulled out his card then slid it across the counter.

"Okay???" The clerk glanced non-challantly at the information.

"Please ma'am, this poor woman is in dire need of seeing her children. Why are you standing in the way of that? You can look at her and see she's distressed... won't you please help her?" Ralph rubbed Roxanne's shoulder.

"Rules are rules." The woman continued typing.

"But what kind of rules prevent a mother from seeing her own children? I mean really..."

"I understand all that but there is still a process you need to follow. We can't just let everyone come in all at once without following the proper protocol in place. Like I said, rules are rules and those are our standards."

"But what would it hurt, just this one time, if you made an exception? I mean, put yourself in her shoes... What about her parental rights?"

"She forfeited those when she dropped them off." The clerk stared blankly at Ralph then looked back at the computer screen.

"But how can she follow the process when you won't even give her a chance in the first place? That alone seems so unfair. Look, I understand she dropped them off and the admittance process has already started, but this organization still has a duty of care and a legal obligation to provide care for families under your program, which also includes some form of parental rights. Especially under the emergency conditions of her unique situation and the desperation of doing whatever she had to in order to get her children some form of shelter and safety.

It's not like she wanted to... this poor family is a victim flooded out due to the storm. Come on, all's I'm asking is if you could just show a little mercy and compassion for this woman and her children. It would do her a world of good just to see them and for the children to see their mother. How could you not see that?"

"Let them through." A voice appeared out of nowhere as a female executive entered from the back office.

"But I thought..." The clerk objected.

"I *said* let them through." The woman reiterated as the clerk pressed the button behind the counter and released the automatic locks.

"Told you to keep the faith..." Ralph reached for Roxanne's hand and smiled as they followed the woman down the long corridor toward the day room.

"Mama!!!" The group of children ran up and hugged their mother one by one in a flurry of love.

"My babies, I've missed you so much!!!" Roxanne fell to her knees as they gathered around her and sat on the floor.

"We thought you were never coming back." The youngest looked up, his eyes filled with tears as the rest of the children chimed in.

"Who are you?" The eldest son stared at Ralph, his eyes filled with curiosity as he sat in the background.

"You can call me friend, but my name is Ralph." He reached out and shook the young man's hand.

"When are we coming home?" Another voice piped up from the small crowd.

"We're working on that now." Ralph tugged at the youngsters curly locks as he looked around at the group of beautiful souls elated to reconnect with their mother.

"Time's up." A voice boomed over the loud speaker.

"Don't go mama... PLEASE DON'T GO!!!" The youngest threw his arms around Roxanne's neck as the others crowded around taking turns hugging and kissing her goodbye.

"When are you coming back?" Another voice rose from the tear filled emotional group of children.

"She'll be back, don't worry." Ralph assured the heartbroken children as they exited hesitantly.

*****

"I can't thank you enough." Roxanne wiped her eyes as they sat at the corner table in the tiny cafe. "It's been a whole week and I still haven't been able to stop crying."

"No need to thank me." Ralph smiled gently and ripped open the envelope.

"What is it?" She looked up from her meal filled with curiosity as he pulled out an information packet.

"It's a work program application for janitorial services in the downtown restaurant and hotel district. I spoke with some good folks over at the Salvation Army and turns out they just opened up a new halfway house for battered women. You can start working this week and stay there until you get back on your feet - I already got you a room and it's just right down the streets so you can see your children whenever you want. "

"I still can't believe it. You have been such a blessing to my family. God bless you." She dropped her head in inexplicable appreciation.

"No worries... and as an added perk, once you work for six months you automatically qualify for a petition to request a pardon from the judge. As long as you have the paperwork, a work history and pass the background check and proof of room and board."

"But can they be allowed to stay at the facility for battered women with me until I save up for a security deposit on an apartment rental?"

"Well... here's the thing - once you have a proven track history that you are in stable condition and a position to provide for your family, I should be able to pull some strings with the Housing Authority to get you into a small rental on the East side of town in the residential district and you can bring your children back home."

"*I can't believe this!!!*" Roxanne threw her arms in the air and fell back into her seat.

"Is everything okay?" A waitress rushed over to the table.

"It's okay..." Ralph assured. "Those are happy tears, she's crying for joy."

Chapter 12

Bryant finished smoothing the fresh concrete with the leveling tool until it was even. It was hard keeping his mind off Brenda with all that had happened but he knew she meant him no good no matter how hard she tried to convince him to take her back. Everyone had been right about her... all she ever wanted was his money. An empty feeling settled in his gut as he reconciled himself with the truth and unsavory images floating around in his head.

How could she have possibly been so untrue? The constant never-ending question tortured his mind daily, especially with all he had done to please her. He had given her everything but the shirt off his back and would have given that too, had only she asked. He had always looked out for her and put her needs before his own. Her wish was his command. He quickly shrugged off the negative thoughts and tried to snap himself out of it as he packed away his tools, then sat on the old metal bench by the fire hydrant to survey the drying cement.

"Is this seat taken?" A soft voice whispered from behind.

"Pardon me?" He quickly glanced over his shoulder slightly thrown off guard, immediately captivated by her stunning beauty.

"Sorry, didn't mean to intrude." A gentle smile eased across the mellow woman's sultry lips. "Mind if I sit here?"

"My pleasure." Bryant soaked in her smooth carmel complexion and long jet black hair.

"I saw you working and all the construction cones so I wasn't sure..." She walked around and slid next to him on the bench.

"It's all good." He gazed over at the gorgeous feminesse then quickly looked away.

"Beautiful sight." She looked up at the dreamy blue sky as the melodious rythm of birds chirped in the background.

"You most certainly are. I mean, yes - it most definitely is..." He smirked, then glanced back at the wet concrete.

"Thanks... I think." She snickered. "And you're quite the handsome gent, if I must say so myself..." She shifted her gaze in his direction, entranced by his rugged good looks. "So how long have you been in construction?"

"Too long, if you ask me." He chuckled to himself then checked his watch. "Just kidding. I been in it for quite a while now, say about twenty years. It just gets a little monotonous when it comes to projects like these - it's like watching paint dry, literally."

"I'll take your word, Bryant." She glanced at his badge.

"I was named after my father." He nodded his head and smiled. "So where's your badge?" He took in her curvy figure beneath the denim jumpsuit.

"Believe it or not, it's the first thing I take off when I leave the office." She unzipped her purse and pulled out the plastic identification card.

"Nice pic, Miss Crystal." He quickly skimmed the name.

"This mugshot?" She giggled and stuck it back inside her leather handbag.

"I beg to differ." He winked. "So what's your line of employment?"

"Thanks, I work at the records department at University Hospital."

"Nice."

"It has its ups and downs, I guess. I mean, it can get a little hectic from time to time but it pays the bills."

"I can relate to that." Bryant glanced back at the wet concrete. "So you're on lunch or what?"

"Let's just say a well needed break." She glanced at her watch.

"I see..." A vision flashed in the back of his mind as he tried to ignore the sting of betrayal.

"Hey, you okay?" She gently nudged his shoulder.

"Just thinking..." His mood slightly shifting as he leaned back to collect his thoughts.

"I'm an awesome listener if that helps any, just saying." She took in his handsome profile and neatly faded hair cut.

"What can I say, *life* I guess."

"It's definitely a journey, I can attest to that. Sometimes I like to take a long stroll on my break just to clear my thoughts. Catch a breath of fresh air and gain a new perspective on whatever it is I'm going through at the current moment."

"You're a deep thinker, I see." The handsome gentleman complimented.

"I think we all have that inner ability when it comes to certain issues of life, especially when it comes to complex situations pertaining to ourselves."

"You seem like you've got a pretty good head on your shoulders though, so I'm sure you're equipped to handle it... whatever it is. I know one thing though, he's a lucky man." Bryant stole another glance at her feminine silhoutte.

"He is?" Crystal looked around. "I'll sure be glad when I meet him."

"Wow, is it like that?"

"Let's just say I'm doing me for now."

"You're kind of comical and I'm sure it's not the first time you've heard that."

"I mean, I might got a few jokes here and there.." She snickered under her breath.

"Oh you got way more than a few?" Timoty teased back.

"Okay, so now who's got the jokes?"

"I'm just saying, beautiful as you are, you can't tell me some young and vibrant suitor has yet to choose a queen like you."

"Actually I've been single for about a good year now, since my break up."

"Wow, sorry to hear that."

"It is what it is, I guess... So how about you?" Crystal inquired curiously.

"Pretty much the same here... Separated."

"My condolences."

"I know right, it's the termination of a marriage. Trust, there is nothing easy when it comes to relationships."

"I think it just all depends on the two individuals and how they relate to one another. Respect and understanding goes a long way. You'll be surprised." Crystal reached in her tote and pulled out a bottle of water and took a sip.

"And that's the first time I've ever heard those words spoken from a female. Are you serious right now?" Bryant looked up in disbelief. "My man was definitely in the winner's seat. You're the one that got away... on the real."

"I guess he's cool with it. We basically just couldn't see eye to eye for some reason."

"I think it's okay to have differences of opinions or outlooks when it comes to certain things, but when it comes to key matters there needs to be some type of similarities within the belief system or it's gonna crash." Ralph reasoned.

"Exactly, and this is the first time I have ever heard that spoken from a male's perspective, so she sounds like the fortunate one."

"If fortunate and money are the same thing, then I guess..." He snorted sarcastically.

"Doesn't sound too good when you put it that way."

"I'm definitely not a bargain type of guy. I believe in going all out for the woman I love but everything shouldn't be a contest of how much you can spend in a matter of seconds or how deep your pockets are."

"Absolutely not.. As they say, the love of money is the root of all evil." Crystal agreed.

"Hey, don't get me twisted. It's nothing wrong with a little wining and dining, I may have a tough exterior, but I'm like a hopeless romantic at heart, like you just said. And it's not the money in itself, it's when you start worshipping it that brings on all of the problems. So it just wasn't a good situation among other things and there were trust issues. I could go further but I'll just leave it at that for now." Ralph looked away

"I feel you. So what you do for fun?"

"Hey, I'm down for whatever. Movies, bowling, dancing... little sky diving here and there." He flicked his collar.

"Sky who?"

"I'm just kidding. I do like to have fun, though. I'm what you call versatile, matter fact, when was the last time you took in a comedy show and had a really good laugh?"

"It's been a minute but I could most definitely stand one right about now, I will tell you that."

"Check it out. A cousin of mine has a friend who sponsors different events at the East Side Theater once a month. You should check it out with me, sometimes." He handed her a business card. "Just tell them, Bryant sent you so you can get in for free. Bring a friend if you like and my number's on the back."

"Thanks." Crystal smiled and headed back to work.

*****

Bryant sat back on the bench and tried to relax, still haunted by the ghosts of his past. He could feel the sadness creeping back in as his heart pounded against his chest. Crystal was fine but he still missed Brenda, although deep inside he knew it was never meant to be and that life would never be the same again without her. That beautiful smile and goofy laugh, the way she wore her hair. She was truly one of a kind but never a keeper because the trust was destroyed. All of the time they had invested was ruined. He thought to himself as he took a final glance at the pavement then packed up his gear and headed toward the truck. It had been a long grueling shift, he recapped the day as he climbed behind the wheel and headed home for a delicious meal and a refreshing night of laughter and relaxation.

*****

The evening sky was filled with romance as Crystal slid into her backless pantsuit and danced to the intoxicating beat as she prepared for a night out on the town. It was an exhilarating sign of new beginnings and the feeling was good, she looked in the mirror and checked her reflection then smoothed on some shimmering lip gloss. Bryant was just what the doctor had ordered to cure her specific case of the blues, in a prescription of strong, handsome allure. Crystal found herself smiling as she thought back to his charming ways and calming exterior of unbridled masculinity then grabbed her keys and headed out the door.

It was the perfect night for romance, she smiled in anticipation as she coasted toward the downtown comedy club joint and pulled up to the parking lot, then pulled out her cellphone and texted the number on the back of the card.

"I'm here..." She typed out the message as the ringtone vibrated, then picked up the call.

"Hey-Hey." Bryant's deep throaty voice drifted from the other end.

"Well hello..." Crystal tingled with excitement.

"Where you at?" He looked around in anticipation. "I'm out by the side entrance in the black Tesla." He let down the tinted window and glanced in the side mirror as the ice blue pearl Transam peeled up next to him.

"Greetings." Crystal purred from behind the wheel.

"And greetings to you too, beloved." Bryant leaned back for a second and checked out her striking appearance then checked out the top of the line sports coupe.

"Catch me if you can." She pulled up next to his spiffy ride and stepped out.

"You definitely wasn't playing, I see." He combed her curvaceous figure tucked inside the snazzy pantsuit and winked.

"You neither." She watched closely as he hopped out the car, his ripped physique decked in a crispy pair of designer jeans and T-shirt.

"After you." Bryant escorted her to the entrance as the doorman gave a welcoming nod, accompanying her to the VIP section of the auditorium as she rambled through her purse and pulled out the entrance pass from earlier. "No need, I got this." He winked. "And you look absolutely gorgeous, by the way." He gestured in appreciation as he made his way to the table and pulled out her seat, then flagged down the waiter.

"Thank you and you are the Dapper Don as usual."

"Cut it out, you're making me blush." He teased as the host made his way to the table.

"Good evening and what can I get for you two?" He pulled out his pen and pad.

"Have it your way babygirl." Bryant glanced down at the menu then back at Crystal.

"Well, I guess I'm not really hungry, but I will take a cocktail."

"Go for it."

"I'd like a bottle of vintage Don Perignon." Crystal leaned back and crossed her legs as she looked around the lavishly furnished surroundings.

"Good taste." Bryant pulled out his wallet and reached for a credit card.

"No need, *I got this*." Crystal pulled out her credit card and handed it to the waiter.

"Now that's definitely the first time I heard those words come out of a woman's mouth, for sure." He cleared his throat and glanced at Crystal then back at the waiter.

"Hey, it's a first time for everything, right?" She winked as they waited for the show to begin.

"Thank you, my Queen." Bryant reached across the table and pressed his palm to hers then kissed the back of her hand as the opening act hit the stage.

"Always welcome." Crystal beamed from within. "What's wrong?"

"It's just been a long time..." He studied the floor in deep thought.

"Let me guess... a long time since you smiled right?"

"You read my mind, how'd you guess?"

"It's probably gonna take some getting used to but I understand. Trust me, I got some emotional baggage of my own but it's okay, this is a No-Rush Zone."

"Yes it is." Bryant looked across the table with a twinkle of hope in his eye and a fresh new perspective he hadn't experienced in years. "You are definitely unique and you are blowing my mind, also?"

"Not to mention, this is the first time I'm reaching into my pocket like this also, so you definitely must be blowing my mind." Crystal laughed.

"You're wild lady, you know that?" Bryant chuckled and enjoyed the moment as he felt the tension ease.

"One of our very best vintage bottles of Don Perignon in the house." The waiter appeared and popped open the bubbly, filling the glasses to the rim. "Awesome choice... may I add... would there be anything else?"

"Hey, what can I say, she's a lady with class." Bryant nodded. "Thanks my man, we good."

"There you go... Hey, sometimes you just gotta say to heck with it and laugh at the world..." She gazed into his handsome face, his brown eyes melting her to the core. "Seems like we both have a lot of healing to do. So let's just lean back and enjoy the ride. Deal?"

"Hey, I'm game if you game." Bryant raised his glass in a toast. "Deal."

"Here's to new beginnings." Crystal tipped her glass as the stage lit up and the band began to play.

*****

"I know this can't be who I think it is." Ralph tossed a few cans into the heavy duty plastic bag and took a few steps back as he did a double take, staring in disbelief.

"And just who do you think it is?"

"Bryant?"

"That's my name, don't wear it out." He met Ralph's hand with a High-Five.

"Man, that's a million dollar smile you're wearing, if I had your hand I'd trade mine in."

"Awe, thanks man... I ain't raisin' no sand. You're looking kind of fly yourself, these days." Bryant returned the compliment.

"If I didn't know any better, I would have thought you was one of those top models. What in the world happened?" Ralph gazed in admiration.

"Hey, I met a beautiful young lady and she turned my world completely around. It's like we just automatically clicked. What can I say, she's good to me."

"*I see.*"

"She's like the yin to my yang, if you dig what I'm saying."

"I heard that, hey ain't nothing wrong with it. Blessings come in many forms."

"I never thought it could happen to me, you know. Especially after all Brenda put me through..." Bryant looked away in deep thought for a moment as he reflected on the past. "But here I am. I can't lie man, I'm having the time of my life for the first time in my life. It's like she understands the simple things in life. You know, she takes time out of her day to pick a few dandelions and even smell the roses. She doesn't let the weeds in life affect her."

"Nothing like dandelions and roses, man." Ralph chuckled.

"Hey, what more can I say? She makes me smile even on a rainy day and even when I'm having a bad day... she makes it good. When I feel like I had it up to here, she takes time out to listen to me... and understand me. She knows how to let a man be a man without compromising who she is as a woman, if you can relate."

"Oh me oh my! You just might wanna get that statement patented."

"I'm already knowing." Bryant snickered.

"Man, do you know how many men would give their everything just to claim they had a woman like that?"

"Yes sir, especially when you've been betrayed in the past like I have and your trust levels are running on empty. I felt like I could never love again, like I could never let down my guard to ever trust again."

"And look at you now, shining like a brand new star."

"Hey, just between me and you, when Brenda put me through all of that madness I went through a really dark season. My head wasn't right for a long time."

"And how could you not have felt blindsided, especially when you truly believed in your heart that you had finally found real love and the very person you trust lets you down in such a devastating way like she did. Sometimes in life though, we have to get drenched by the rain before we can enjoy the sunshine." Ralph spoke words of wisdom.

"Man, I gave that woman everything I had and it's like it was never enough."

"You can't buy love, son."

"And I wasn't trying to. I just wanted to supply her with the things she wanted... please her. Please her and satisfy her needs, why is that so wrong?"

"It's not as long as you're equally yoked and appreciated. See, love has to be reciprocated. It's not a one sided-thing. True love is generous and kind - it's not a one way street. Love is trusting and forgiving. Understanding and compassionate. It does not abuse and take advantage nor is it greedy or prideful. Whenever those elements are present it serves as a red flag and can become a breeding ground for betrayal."

"I guess I just had to learn the hard way." Bryant's head swirled with flashbacks as they played back and forth in his mind on repeat. "Even now I still find myself thinking about her so I guess the pain will never fully go away. She really did a number on me." He reconciled himself with the truth.

"There are definitely some events in our lives that we will never fully heal from or comprehend and although we may learn to walk again, there will always be a subtle limp. Sometimes major, depending on how treacherous the offense. Some emotional wounds last far longer than any physical scar ever will."

"Your wisdom runs deep." Bryant welcomed his wealth of knowledge in admiration as Ralph breathed more words of life.

"And Proverbs 4;23 tells us to *"Guard Your Heart With All Diligence, For Out Of It Flows The Issues Of Life."* It is the Book Of Wisdom. Always remember that, son."

"Thanks for everything, I probably wouldn't even be standing here had it not been for you, man." Bryant reached out and shook his hand.

"No worries... hey, I'm truly happy for you. Crystal's a fine woman, both inside and out. You've done well."

"Wait a minute, that's crazy... how did you know her name?" Bryant froze in shock.

"You wouldn't by any chance be talking about the Crystal who works over at the University in the file department, now would you?" Ralph smiled cunningly and winked.

"So you do know her."

"Would it make a difference if I did, I mean as long as you're happy, right?" Ralph's smirk grew a little wider... "And you are happy aren't you?"

"Very. As a matter of fact, I haven't been this happy in a long time... For years in all actuality. I can't even remember the last time I laughed and enjoyed myself like that it's been so long."

"Then that's all that matters. You deserve it, son. See you around." Ralph patted him on the back and headed to his car.

Chapter 13

"I woke up one morning and I didn't hate him anymore." The administrative head spoke frankly as she directed Ralph down the long hallway toward her office and closed the door.

"Wow, just like that?" He took a seat as she made her way around the desk and sat down.

"Well, it definitely took a lot of prayer and then some. In addition to the fact that someone thought enough to lay hands on me, which I'm convinced had everything to do with this colossal turn of events in my life. Especially, in comparison from where I started to where I sit today. The transition has been quite miraculous, to say the least. Another major cornerstone has also been the kindness and generosity you have shown me - that saved my life. I don't know how I could ever repay you for what you have done for me. Had you not stepped in when you did, I probably wouldn't be standing here today. The pain was literally eating me alive."

"You have no idea what seeing you flourish like this does for me - it's priceless. Way beyond it's weight in gold. That's my payment. It was really heartbreaking seeing you in the streets like that. I knew you were destined for so much more." Ralph glanced at the stack of files on her desk and the fancy name plate. "Thanks for inviting me up, it was so good running into you today. To be honest, I never thought I'd see you again."

"Yes, I pretty much hit rock bottom when he betrayed me and out of all people, he did it with my best friend. But the anger I had stored up inside was doing more harm to me than it was to anyone else and I had to face that fact, once and for all."

"Sweet music to my ears beloved, you've come a long-long way."

"Yes sir, I have. After I completed the program I felt extremely inspired to make a change. I knew from all the torment, pain and suffering I had endured and overcome that I could help somebody else. Reach someone and let them know that they are not alone in their struggle. Maybe offer some guidance to keep someone from doing something they would regret for the rest of their life.

So after I enrolled myself into the program, they actually paid for me to go back to school and I will tell you from the bottom of my heart that being a principal and also a guidance counselor for this younger generation is the most fulfilling work I have ever done in my life. You'd be surprised how eager these students are to put in the hard work to prepare for a brighter future, especially the at-risk juniors and undergrads who often have external challenges from home or family circumstances. Believe me, there is no greater reward than seeing the fruits of your labor when you know you have made a difference in someone's life.

"Every day I see the look in these young people's eyes. The

sadness. The need to know that someone somewhere cares. And the fear that no one does.... and it just rips me apart." She stood up and led him out into the hall as they walked from room to room. "This school is filled with who some may call juvenile delinquents, but I disagree. I believe these are adolescents from all walks of life and adverse situations who were dealt an extremely difficult hand from the very beginning. Many of them came into this world with people turning their backs on them. The emotional scars on their hearts and minds can never be erased but our goal is to create some type of buffer between them and this world. Give them at least a fighting chance to get the proper education and tools they need to succeed in mainstream society. Our goal is to pick them up where this world dropped them off.

"When my husband betrayed me with who I thought was my best friend, it shattered me to pieces. I felt so low in life and so abandoned. It triggered a need in me to want to help anybody else who had been rejected and let them know that someone cares, because I know how that feels.

"It may not be an easy job, but it's definitely a worthwhile one." Her eyes burned with conviction and compassion as she walked the halls in a classy beige Ralph Lauren business suit. Her carefully coiffed hair pulled into a sophisticated bun and the tiny diamond stud earrings framing her beautiful face, a paradoxical contradiction of the shattered woman he had met months before crouched on the ground, hiding beneath the raggedy oversized coat.

"No offense, but... " Ralph followed her in total disbelief, taken aback by her eloquent appearance. "It's hard to believe you're even the same person. It's like you're glowing from within. Your spirit, the look in your eyes and your skin... A total transformation."

"And I can't thank you enough." She stopped at the first classroom on the lower level of the building and opened the door. "No worries, I'm just conducting a tour." She peeked in first and reassured the instructor, then escorted Ralph throughout the brightly lit Resource Room.

"I've never seen students looking so happy and jubilent. Eager to learn." Ralph followed her back out into the hallway as she closed the door and covered her face.

"Why the tears?" Ralph reached out to grab her hand as he gathered his composure.

"You don't understand - these students have an everlasting place in my heart. The strength and determination alone on a day-to-day basis, just to get up and face another day when everything around them is working against them, yet they keep pushing on. The dedication they have and the thirst to become the best that they can be and fulfill the gift God put in their little hearts. Despite what the world says about them, they still refuse to give up." She pulled a tissue from her pocket and wiped the tears from her eyes. "Despite what they have endured in life, there remains that little touch of innocence that still wants to believe that there is some good left in this world."

"Believe it or not, those beautiful little souls in there were written off by the world and the system, but not by God. It tears me apart to believe that anyone would do such a thing to the most innocent, troubled and vulnerable of society. Yet, that's the world we're living in today. Can you believe that? Because I can't." She glanced back through the window as the lively group of children chattered heartily as they moved from resource station to station. "These children were given up on before they even had a chance and it breaks my heart every day."

"You would never believe it from their inner spirit." Ralph looked around the brightly furnished room. "The work you do here is amazing. This world would be surprised to see just what a little patience, understanding and a touch of love will do. If only more people thought like you and we could just give one another a chance, instead of writing each other off because of our narrow minded viewpoints and judgemental opinions of what we deem as different - the world would be an awesome place. She strengthened her reserve then headed toward the next classroon and opened the door as a group of children exercised on a mat, while another group rolled a medicine ball back and forth. Then joined in on a quick game of catch and toss as she threw the tiny beanbag into a bucket before they made their way back into the hall.

"Contrary to popular belief, a good therapeutic treatment plan and a consistant overall structured program for each individual's needs would make a marked difference over time and most, if not all, could overcome the odds or make significant progress. These are the true geniuses of our time." She headed toward another classroom and cracked the door as a room full of students looked down at their desks, studying attentively. "All of these students had to be retested on their standerdized exams consecutively for three to five years straight. Once accepted into this program, they are now known as the next mathematician and science wizards of the next generation according to their outstanding test scores.

"Each one of them can match minds and talents with some of the most brilliant mathematic and science scholars in the nation. In fact, many of them are already working at entry level positions within those fields and are being mentored by some of the top virologists, geometricians, staticians and calculus instructors at some of the top tier universities and medical institutions citywide.

According to their performance and state rankings by the time they graduate and pass the entrance exame - many of them will already have clear path to apply, and if all goes well, get accepted into entry level engineering positions throughout the math, medical, science and physics top notch statewide programs and institutions across the board." Her eyes filled with inspiration as she looked around the room. "You are looking at some of the greatest minds of the next generation and to think that they were all written off by society.

"Many of these very students have also experienced trauma, lack, familial and betrayal issues and environmental triggers. They know the pain when it comes from the inside and the very people you once believed in let you down along with the world around you. We're taught that people close to us, friends and family, are supposed to have your back... but in life we often find out that isn't the case. One of the worst kinds of betrayals in the world is by the hands of someone you trust. But that devastation, that pain and that struggle birthed these little heroes. Propelled them toward greatness. They are not only brilliant but they are also resilient and we are so very proud of them." The principal closed the door as they headed down the long corridor. "And to address your previous comment, you could never offend me." She turned and faced Ralph eye to eye.

"I could have never done this without you. You turned my world around and changed the entire trajectory of my path. When life wrote me off and my husband, who I took vows with and committed to matrimony as a loving wife, cooking, cleaning, helping with the bills and pitching in however I could to have his back betrayed me for no reason at all - you were there. Do you know what it's like to love someone so much that you give them everything you have and they throw it all away like waste?

But you stepped in and picked me up, kept me from giving up, brushed me off and put me back together again. You stepped in and brightened the way. Taught me to trust when I never believed I could trust again... and I thank you kindly, sir."

"God showed you all those things. He is the One who kept you strong when no one else was there. He is the One who picked you up and dusted you off and dried your tears when you cried yourself to sleep at night.... I'm just the vessel." Ralph wrapped his arm around her shoulder as they headed out of the building.

"May I hinder you for just one more favor." She followed him out into the parking lot.

"But of course." Ralph stopped and faced her eye to eye.

"Please, don't ever change..."

"I think I can grant you that... on one condition."

"Of course..." She smiled as she faced him eye to eye.

"Promise to never stop believing..."

"I PROMISE..." She hugged him and waved then headed back

inside the building as he made his way to his car.

Chapter 14

A crack of sunlight from the early morning haze seeped through the blinds as Vicky peeked over the blanket. The sedative had worn off and it was a new day, she thought to herself as she looked around the small corner space.

"Feeling alot better, I hope." A nursing assistant peeked inside then walked over and sat on the edge of the bed to take her temperature.

"I owe you all everything." She reached out and hugged the kind woman.

"You're all good." Her eyes filled with hope and compassion as she gave Vicky a quick squeeze then glanced back at the thermometer. "Any plans for the day?"

"Just plan on getting out for a while I guess. You know, clear my thoughts - get my head right."

"I know that's right. Hey, go have some fun for a change, just try not to get too right, if you know what I mean. Just teasing, you know I'm rooting for you I just want you to stay out of trouble, that's all." She gave her another quick squeeze and exited.

"I will and thanks again." Vicky reassured her then hopped in the shower, threw on some gear and headed across the boulevard toward the small cafe diner, her mind a maze of confusion as she went inside.

"May I help you?" Audrey continued wiping down the countertops without looking up.

"Hi, I'm just coming back to check on my application." She walked to the counter and sat down.

"And you are?" Audrey looked up non-challantly, her voice cold and aloof.

"Hey, it's me - Vicky. Don't you remember me?"

"Sorry, we get so many people coming in and out it's pretty hard to keep up with the names." She continued wiping.

"I mean like really, come on you've gotta be kidding me. This is all just one big joke right, you're pulling my leg or what? How can you even part your lips to say you don't remember me when you're the one who suggested I apply in the first place. And now you're looking me directly in my face telling me you don't even remember me? I'm confused."

"Like I said, I see so many faces it's just impossible to keep up." Audrey placed the dishtowel on the counter then picked up the broom and started sweeping.

"So you don't even remember telling me about the help needed for the evening shift the other day? You actually gave me an application and I filled it out. You were going to reach out to the manager because I didn't have the main number to the Salvation and you specifically told me not to worry because you knew some people over there. Am I going crazy or what?" Vicky stared in confusion.

"Only you can answer that one, dear." Audrey rolled her eyes and set the broom aside, then grabbed a few cannisters and began filling them with cream and sugar.

"Hey, if I am I'm not by myself, that's for sure."

"Listen ma'am, I don't want any trouble so I'm gonna have to ask you to leave the premises." Audrey reached for the phone.

"I already told you my name, plus it's also on the application so you cut it with the ma'am. It really makes me wonder if you even kept it on file. Wasn't it you who gave me the pep talk about staying strong, in the first place? I confided in you that I'm going through a very difficult season and trying to get back up on my feet - and now all of a sudden you can't even remember my name or face?" Vicky slid back from the counter in dismay.

"I honestly don't remember that conversation, I'm sorry." Audrey picked up a fresh package of styrofoam cups and stacked them on the counter.

"May I have the number to the corporate office, please?" Vicky reached into her belt bag for an ink pen.

"Hang on, you do look slightly familiar now that I think about it." Audrey dropped what she was doing and eased back over to the counter.

"Now we're getting somewhere." Vicky played along. "So, what's the verdict?"

"I'm not saying it's written in stone, but last I heard the position had already been filled." She pushed up her bifocals and continued working.

"Why so many games, you can see I need help. Can't you contact someone?"

"I'm afraid that's beyond my reach." Audrey turned abruptly and left the counter.

"Please, I'll cook, clean, wash dishes - whatever it is you need me to do. I just really need a job... couldn't you reach out to the manager?"

"That's entirely up to you ma'am, I have no idea what the number is." Audrey looked unbothered as a group of afternoon patrons entered. "Well, gotta get back to work now, take care." She forced a smile then rushed off to greet the incoming customers as Vicky waited patiently, then exited the diner and headed down the bleary avenue. The sun was shining outside but inside her heart was covered in darkness, she dried her tears as she glanced at the replacement flip phone the Salvation had given her and checked the status bar. Then quickly turned it back off to preserve the battery.

Everything was a mess, she studied the ground as she walked along the boulevard, contemplating the many ways she could finally bring an end to the suffering and stop the misery once and for all. She deliberated in silence, quietly easing into the tiny family owned independent business as she sized up the environment. Then slipped into the basement and hid behind a stack of boxes loaded beneath the crawl space until morning.

A feeling of worthlessness and despair sunk in the pit of her stomach as she waited patiently for the owners to reopen shop at the crack of dawn, then quickly dipped back out into the streets. Humiliated in shame, besieged by the frowns from the early morning work crowd and their contemptuous scowls. *Maybe they were right all along.* Vick reasoned to herself as she glanced in the window at her tired reflection and tattered clothing, then reached for the main entrance door of the Salvation and headed toward the food counter in the day room.

"Well looky here." Carlotta folded her arms across her chest and snarled from the back of the line. "So we finally decided to woman up and face the music, hey? You just might even have some heart, after all."

"I have nothing to prove to you or anyone else." Vicky felt a rush as she finally stood up to her longstanding nemesis. "I'm not the same person you once knew."

"Says who?"

"Look, I'm just doing what I have to do in order to get out of here as quickly as possible."

"Who isn't?" Carlotta smirked mischievously.

"I can't answer for anyone else, all I can do is speak for myself."

"And you came up with that all on your own, I guess."

"I'm just stating the facts." Vicky stood her ground.

"This is not a game, it's real life and it's real simple. If you can't beat 'em then you may as well join 'em. So you can either roll with me or get rolled over, choice is yours." Carlotta continued to harass.

"Hey, I just prefer to stay away from anything immoral. The last thing I need is to land in more hot water." Vicky could feel her resistance waning fast, but she also knew that going against Carlotta would come with a steep price. She didn't stand a chance and she knew it. They were from two different worlds and she didn't have the rank nor the pull to call her bluff.

"Immoral is such a harsh word. I prefer *unconscionable*,

personally. It just seems a lot less abrasive and judgemental, but that's just my opinion. How about we look at this as more of a business opportunity." Carlotta glanced over at her remorseless cronies, then back at Vicky. "Let's face it, from the looks of things you've already got your work cut out with these winners, so it's a win-win situation in your case. Especially if you're not from where I come from. At least with me, I'll cut you a tad bit more slack because in this place, you're definitely gonna need some protection and that's the mild version if you really want the truth. Like I said earlier, it's really not a game, sweetie."

"I may not be from your neck of the woods but that doesn't necessarily mean I'm an idiot, either."

"That doesn't really matter if everyone else sees you as one, though. This place doesn't operate on a workbook format like in grade school. *Alice in Wonderland*, this is not." Carlotta leveled the playing field.

"I just like to play by the rules and stay away from as much negativity as possible."

"It has nothing to do with being negative or having a questionable character - it's a matter of doing what it takes to survive. You really think some good samaritan is just gonna spring up out of nowhere and come rescue you from all this? What's in your morning cappuccino?"

"You don't have to talk down to me."

"All I'm saying is you can keep sitting on your hands if you like and you'll be waiting until the cows come home... if they ever do." Carlotta patted Vicky on the shoulder and winked.

"I'd rather graze with the cows then squabble with the pigs any day of the week." Vicky retorted.

"Have it your way, but you're really starting to aggravate me, you know that right?"

"Why is that?"

"I mean you talk all this good game and all, yet look where you ended up." Carlotta looked around the homeless shelter then back at Vicky. "So tell me, where exactly has it gotten you?"

"I just prefer to play it safe, so sue me."

"Don't tempt me." Carlotta snickered. "Seriously, there's a stiff penalty for ignorance, always has and always will be."

"There's also penalties for being conniving." Vicky countered.

"Look, we can go back and forth all day - the bottom line is comparing facts won't get either one of us out of this situation. So, I heard you were looking for work."

"All depends..." Vicky concentrated on Carlotta's words for a moment.

"On what?"

"What type of work you're referring to?"

"So glad you asked." Carlotta reached in her pocket and pulled out the crinkled up flyer and unfolded it.

"They're hiring over at the old factory right off the Boulevard. It might not be top dollar but it's definitely something to hold you down for the time being. And if at all possible, a little appreciation kick-back would be greatly appreciated once you get on, if you wouldn't mind." Carlotta giggled sarcastically.

"I don't know, isn't that in one of the roughest areas in town?" Vicky glanced at the flyer and quickly handed it back.

"You're a big girl, I'm sure you can handle it." Carlotta shoved the employment advertisement away. "You'll never get anywhere in life if you don't take chances."

"No guarantees but I'm listening." Vicky straightened her posture.

"It goes far beyond listening, you gotta be smart and recognize when someone is trying to help you. Know how to take advantage of a good opportunity instead of sleeping on it. They even offer a sign on bonus and if that's not an incentive, I don't know what is."

"Okay, I'm smart - I'm *smart*."

"Let's not overdo it. I'm simply reiterating the fact that anyone can claim to be a trillionaire but that still won't put one thin dime in your bank account, unless you're willing to do the work. Period. No one is going to hold your hand."

"True."

"So you want out of this predicament or not? Either way, don't waste my time."

"I'm just speechless, I guess. We started out on such a rough course and to see things turn around for the good is almost unbelievable. I just never thought, out of all people -" Vicky felt herself growing emotional as she looked down at the job opportunity leaflet.

"That I would be the one to help you, right?"

"Exactly."

"Hey, one for the team, as they say. Charge it to the game."

"But it's not every day a foe becomes an ally, what made you do it?" Vicky stared at Carlotta perplexedly.

"Who knows, it may be something in it for me, after all. Hey, no good deed goes unpunished, you know?" Carlotta smiled shrewdly. "You seem to be up on the boulevard enough to navigate the seedy areas though. Just remember, never show your fear."

"I pass through from time to time, but I'm sure I'll be okay."

"So you know how to move then, right?"

"Move?"

"Not literally. *Figuratively*." Carlotta chuckled mischievously.

"I'm there for all the after holiday shopping deals and the local county fair."

"I just bet you are."

"The popcorn is great. Anyway, I think I can handle it." Vicky reassured unsuspectingly.

"Purrfect." Carlotta took a seat and waited patiently.

"Maybe I should wait until morning and get a fresh start, though." Vicky reconsidered as she glanced at her watch. "It is getting pretty late and I do recognize the fact it's a whole new ballgame in that vicinity come nightfall."

"I'm sure you'll be just fine. Like you said, you're already familiar with the area so you should have nothing to worry about." Carlotta nudged Vicky along. "Keep in mind spots are filling up quickly so you'll wanna get as much of a jump on the competition as possible. Keep in mind, it's in the same location of that busy section by that one corner store and the new cafe they just built right off the alleyway."

"True." Vicky answered hesitantly as she took a final glance at the address on the flyer.

"I just don't feel good about this, I really do think I should wait until morning." Vicky contemplated.

"What's there to feel good about, it's simple. Walk over there, fill out the paper work and walk away."

"Will you come with me?" Vicky started on her way reluctantly, then stopped and turned around.

"Sorry, I wish I could but you know they got me on a curfew restriction from last month."

"But what if I run into somebody crazy?" Vicky looked up at the evening sky.

"You're looking at a three-hundred dollar pay day. Do you know what that could do for your situation? Hey, you don't wanna miss out on a lifetime opportunity."

"Relax, I got an ear to the streets and I know everybody around here. Trust me my people got you, plus I got eyes everywhere. My watchmen got watchmen. So if anything crazy happens - just tell 'em *Car* sent you and they'll know what to do from there. That's my code name in the streets, short for Carlotta." Carlotta tapped Vicky on the shoulder and gave her a gentle shove. "Now run along, sweetie."

*****

It was Ten o'clock p.m. and the streets were unusually quiet as Vicky walked quickly toward the main boulevard, cautiously casing the environment as a male figure in a grey jacket approached, commanding her attention as he eased toward the alleyway.

"What's up Miss Lady?" A gruff voice spoke over a pair of husky shoulders.

"Car sent me." She stood still, frozen in fear.

"Who?" A wicked grin crossed his face as he turned around with an evil smirk and snatched the application out of her hands.

"Car - Carlotta." She took a few steps back and ran for her life, then dipped through a vacant lot and fled the scene as she scrambled toward the shelter.

The receptionist's booth was closed as she peered inside the dark office area then dashed down the silent corridors toward the tiny area she had been assigned and quickly turned the corner as she slammed into Carlotta.

"Welcome back." Her eyes piercing and cold as she stared through Vicky.

"HE TOOK MY APPLICATION!!!" Vicky shrieked, her body shuddering uncontrollably.

"So let him have it then." Carlotta looked away indifferently.

"You set me up, you had to!" Vicky sobbed hysterically.

"I have no idea what you're talking about." Carlotta turned and headed in the opposite direction.

"You were never my friend to begin, you never changed." Vicky collapsed and fell to the floor as a crowd gathered around, then slipped into the hallway stairwell and out into the darkness of the night. She knew there was no place to hide, she weighed her options as the footsteps behind her gained momentum. Gasping to catch her breath, she ran toward the boulevard under the safety of the street lights as she glanced back over her shoulder at a few lovers strolling in the distance.

She needed something to relax, the psychedelic lights of the neon sign on the convenience store caught her eye as she tipped inside and looked around the crowded space. Then headed for the back of the store toward the neatly lined bottles of iced coffee and grabbed a container and headed to the register.

"I'm so thirsty and I only have a dollar." She reached down into her pocket and grabbed a handful of change and poured it onto the countertop.

"I got you." The attendant nodded his head in compassion.

"God bless you." She slipped the container into her pocket and tipped into the single stall bathroom. Then turned off the lights and popped the cap and emptied the contents into an empty water bottle and scrambled out the door.

The bleak street lights cast a murky glow, streaming a dull path toward the desolate boulevard as Vicky headed back toward the park. A tense silence hung in the air as the faint sound of a barking dog faded in and out as she pulled out the plastic water bottle and gulped it half way down, her nerves immediately soothed by an intensive calm as she floated toward the park bench.

Total darkness covered the evening sky as she watched a few teens playing a game of hoops as they quickly scattered. Checking her surroundings once more, she slowly reached back inside her pocket and pulled out the plastic bottle and gulped down the last of the iced drink. It had been a long time since she had a place to lay her head but she couldn't give up, she dozed off for a moment then came to and sat up on the bench as a dark shadow appeared in her peripherals then faded away.

"Who's there?" A streak of terror raced through her veins as she called into the darkness, gripped in fear. Then quickly hopped off the bench and dashed into a thicket of trees. Her heart banging in her chest, kicking her instincts into high gear as the creepy presence of someone lurking nearby lingered in the distance. An eerie rustling of dry underbrush crunched beneath the sound of footsteps against the lush floor of the forest's surface pierced the air.... drawing closer and closer as she stiffened her body against the woodsy terrain, deadlocked in silence.

"*I know you're in there...*" A creepy male voice whispered. "You know it's only a matter of time before I find you my love, so you may as well save time and come on out." Vicky trembled under the sound of the sinister voice, her body stock-still as a long slippery creature slithered between her thigh and pierced her flesh through the underbelly of crushy weeds as she faded away.

Chapter 15

The brilliant rays of the morning sun peaked through the cluster of trees as Vicky shielded her eyes from the blare. Slowly mustering the strength, she managed to pull forward and sit up, quickly looking around the dense woods as she brushed off a heap of tiny brown bugs and beetles from her swollen skin ravaged in tiny red bite marks.

A blurred vision of wildlife and lush greenery floated in and out as she felt herself lose control, falling backwards into the weeds. Her energy slowly fading away, reeling from the dizziness as she gathered up the courage and rolled to the side, then reached inside her pocket to retrieve the tiny electronic gadget and pressed the power button. A missed call icon lit up the tiny cell phone screen in fluorescent letters as she steadied her shaking hands and pressed the automatic redial button.

"Hello is this Vicky? We've been trying to reach you."

"I need help." She heard herself murmur as she answered the familiar voice. "Listen, I have some great news for you. This is Genievieve from the Young Adult Risk Program and an anonymous donor has just set you up to receive a wonderful gift but we need you to come down here to the facility. It's the same location not too far from the motel, do you remember?"

"Yes, I think so..." Vicky felt herself growing weaker and weaker as she covered the speaker and weeped.

"Great, I'll explain everything once you get here, see ya soon."

"Okay..." Vicky whispered into the receiver.

"Is everything okay???"

"No ma'am, it's not." She pulled herself up and staggered forward then stumbled back to the ground.

"Where are you?... Hello - What's going on???" The facilitator questioned frantically.

"I've been attacked and I need some help."

"Oh my goodness - where are you? I'm gonna call and send a squad car out to you right away. You just stay put. Tell me your location."

"I'm at Albany Park by Saldisbury Road right off the main Boulevard."

"I'll send someone right away - just stay on the line..."

"Yes ma'am." Vicky crawled through the woods toward a small opening in the trees and stretched out across the pavement as the distant sound of sirens filled the air, growing closer and closer until they reached the park. She could hear the sound of rubber peeling on the pavement as they pulled up, followed by the sound of hurried footsteps.

"Everything's okay, we're here now." The stocky built police officer knelt down and placed his arm around her shoulder then lifted up her chin and looked into her eyes as he reached out his hand to help her up.

"I didn't know what was going to happen." Vicky sobbed into his chest as he led her to the car and called for an ambulance.

"I'm just glad we were able to reach you in time - you're extremely blessed." He helped her out of the car as two paramedics lifted her onto the gurney and whisked her away.

*****

The hospital room was peaceful as Vicky lay in the bed, still shivering from the traumatic events as she cried hysterically to herself in the silence. She knew she would never be the same, never be able to erase the pain from her memory, she pondered the frightful events as she covered her face in her hands and sobbed into the darkness. It felt like no one cared and no one ever would. From day one she had been in it alone. She studied the floor questioning her purpose in life for the umpteenth time as the hospital door swung open.

"How are you?" The older woman entered the room and sat down next to her on the bed.

"I want out." The endless tears flowed uncontrollably as she looked up at the ceiling and out of the window. "I hate my life - I don't want to be here anymore... I just want out." She felt her soul draining from her body as she fell back on the bed.

"Please don't talk that way." The kind woman pulled her close and hugged her tight... "Please don't give up."

"GIVE ME ONE REASON TO LIVE!!!" Vicky slid off the side of the bed down to the floor, pulling her knees into her chest as she whimpered in despair.

"But what if I told you that everything was about to change?"

"And what if I told you that I don't believe you?"

"But what if it was true, though?"

"Yeah... okay lady."

"I am so serious."

"Look, I've been lied to enough in life, look at me now."

"Will you come with me?" The kind woman reached out her hand and gently helped up.

"I'm just so tired."

"I know..." She hugged her as tight as she could - infusing as much love as possible."

"Go away from me - I just wanna lay down. Why waste your time, can't you see I'm worthless?"

"No. I will not go away from you... I want to stay with you - I want to help you. Please allow me to help you." The woman pulled back and looked Vicky in her eyes. "Do you believe you are worthy of help? Do you believe that you deserve help? You gotta believe it in your heart, sweetie."

"All I know is that I'm tired."

"Trust and believe me, you are truly not alone and definitely not the only one who feels that way. Been there a time or two myself, you probably need a ticket to get in that line, dear."

"Just leave me alone." Vicky collapsed onto the bed and sobbed.

"Look. I know you're probably sick and tired of me and I do understand. And I promise to obey your wishes and get out of your face, once and for all, if you would just do me this one stinking favor."

"*Please I'll do it - I'll do it.*" Vicky lashed out in exhaustion.

"Come with me - I need to show you something." She grabbed her car keys and led Vicky out the door.

"Why are you torturing me - where are we going???" She climbed into the car and grudgingly sunk into the passenger's seat as they rode through the evening traffic and headed across town, then turned down a beautiful tree-lined street with rows of expensive brick infrastructures.

"I didn't know an area like this even existed in real life." Vicky looked around at the luxurious surroundings. "Where have you taken me and who are your people?" She giggled sarcastically.

"Well, come go with me so we can find out." The social worker hopped out the car and grabbed Vicky's hand and led the way. "Take your time."

"Trust, the pain will definitely remind me." She paused for a second then wobbled a few steps, still ravaged from the traumatic events and the side effects of the sedative as she made her way toward the well maintained yellow brick building with bright green awnings trimmed with beautiful flowers and sprawling green grass. "This looks like the wealthy district where money grows on trees...and lots and lots of it, too." She leaned on the woman's shoulder for support as they clodded toward the door of the upscale building and headed down the long hall clad in plush oriental carpeting and mahogany woodwork.

"Right this way, ma'am." The woman stuck the key in the lock and opened the door to the extravagantly fully furnished condominium. "It's all yours." She waved her hand in a gesture of welcome.

"Huh?" Vicky rubbed her eyes and blinked. "I don't understand, you jiving me or what lady?" She stepped inside, awestruck as she looked around the lavishly furnished condiminium in disbelief.

"Not bad for fresh new beginnings, wouldn't you agree?" She smirked.

"Of course it's beautiful, no doubt... but you know I can't afford something like this. How could I ever pay for all of this?" She looked around at the vaulted ceilings and stainless steel appliances, complete with a leather sectional and big screen television mounted to the wall. "I can't even believe this is real." She gazed out the window at the luxurious landscape surrounded by a beautiful orchard of trees.

"Look woman." The kind lady grabbed a clump of tissue and handed it to Vicky. "I'm switching to the kleenex business if you keep this up."

"These are happy tears!!!" Vicky jumped up and down...."But who did this?"

"Remember I told you an anonymous donor set you up for a gift?....Well this is it. And it's all yours. But here's the real kicker... *It's totally paid for.*" She handed Vicky a slip of paper. "All you need to do is enroll in this remarkable program. They've also made it possible for you to have access to a full scholarship, then once you've earned your Master of Business Administration you are automatically gauranteed a position within the organization starting at top tier salary, which should take care of your rent and necessities - all while giving back and helping others, just like we helped you. What a wonderful way to pay it forward. Sound like a deal?"

"*If This Is A Dream Please Don't Wake Me!!!!*" Vicky fell on the couch in disbelief. "But who did this????" She spun around in circles. "You really have no idea?... Please - I just need to tell them thank you..."

"That's just it, they chose to remain anonymous. It's the strangest thing though, because usually we can always find some sort of record but we can't even trace this donor. It's like they called from out of nowhere, put in an inquiry, viewed it online - then paid it in full. Just like that. Even when we searched for the credit card information after the transaction, in hopes that it would lead us to some contact information so that we also could at least thank them for this tremendous act of kindness, we found that the transaction had been made with some pre-loadable card and the account had been shut down. Soooo, in this case, I'd just say *ENJOY IT*." She smiled and hugged Vicky one last time then handed her the keys and left.

"God Bless you." Vicky echoed appreciatively as she locked the door and continued exploring the high end condominium, from the granite counter tops, stainless steel appliances and elegant ceiling to floor draperies. Then grabbed the remote control and flipped through the channels as Carlotta's mugshot flashed across the screen in a breaking news alert.

"Female bandit detained and arrested in connection with money laundering, theft and conspiracy after a long investigation." Overtaken by a flood of relief, Vicky turned up the volume and listened closely as she closed the final chapter of her past.

Justice had finally been served, Vicky rejoiced as she unlocked the French doors and slid them open. Then stepped outside on the balcony to clear her mind as the gentle evening dew settled on the porch. *Things were finally beginning to change for the better.* She consoled her weary mind as she relaxed and reflected on life under the beautiful skylights from the motel and the majestic glow of the moon. Taking in a breath of fresh air, she could finally feel herself slowly coming back to her senses as a radiant figure from across the way stood off in the distance. His familiar silhouette prompting her memory as his image etched clearer and clearer as Ralph appeared through the evening glimmer.

"Hey you - I've been looking all over the place, where've you been? I just wanted to thank you for getting me set up in the program and everything you've done for me!" Vicky shouted across the gangway into the subtle evening haze, overtaken by joy as the realization finally settled in that it had been him working behind the scenes all along... He had engineered and maneuvered the whole thing. The mastermind and the anonymous donor... but how? Vicky stood on the balcony in amazement as she glanced at her watch then quickly looked back and gasped, astounded in wonderment as Ralph's image slowly diminished... disappearing into thin air as it evaporated in the mist....

It had to be a dream. Vicky slipped on her house shoes and charged down the stairwell, then ran outside searching through the darkness as she raced back inside toward the lobby. "Hey, did anybody see that man standing outside in front of the motel!!!" She bellowed.

"Who???" The desk clerk looked up in bewilderment.

"THAT MAN..." Vicky pointed toward the door. "HE was just standing there... in the parking lot - and now he's GONE!" Vicky ran back outside shouting in disbelief. "WHERE DID HE GO!!!" She shouted to the rooftops.

Chapter 16

It had been a long night, Vicky rubbed her weary eyes as she awoke from the deep trance of the muscle relaxers, hit the shower, got dressed and called for a local cabbie. The irrefutable memories of all that had happened could never be erased. She sat in a trance, steadying herself on the bumpy ride as the driver headed down the boulevard then turned into the gas station parking lot at her request.

"This is all I have." She frantically reached inside her jeans and pulled out her last dollar bill.

"I got it, sweetie." The older man nodded in compassion.

"Thank you!" She hopped out and ran inside, in desperate need of answers. "Please, I need to speak with Roscoe the store manager, is he available - this is serious!" She gasped, fighting to catch her breath.

"I'm sorry." A thin older man spoke from behind the counter. "Roscoe sold the business months ago, it's under new management now." He looked up for a moment and paused, then finished unloading a pallet of boxes.

"Are you serious right now??? Please, I really need to speak with him. He worked with the Young Adult Risk Initiative, they provide jobs for underserved communities and I'm looking for my friend Ralph. He runs the program, do you know him?"

"I'm sorry miss, I wish I could be of more help, but I have no idea who that is and right now the store is being managed directly from corporate until they find a replacement."

"Please - how can I get in touch with the previous manager?"

"I don't have access to previous employee records - only corporate has admittance to those." He turned and headed toward the counter to assist a customer.

"Just forget it then!" Vicky flew out the door and sprinted back to the shelter and headed inside.

"Can I help you?" The unfamiliar clerk continued typing on the computer.

"Please, how can I get in touch with the supervisor, I was just in here a few weeks ago and I'm trying to get in touch with an old resident who's a friend of mine, his name is Ralph."

"Name doesn't jog my memory, sorry." She glanced over the counter then looked away.

"Seriously, I met him some months ago when I first came in here to stay, he helped me get back on my feet."

"Like I said, I have no idea who that is. We don't keep personnel information on file like that and I'm fairly new so I really wouldn't be able to help you. Sorry, wish I could do more."

"Come on, someone's gotta know something."

"Sorry, but that's about all I got." She hopped in her rolling chair and slid back to her desk.

"What about the lunch ladies who work in the cafeteria?"

"Like I said before, we have rotating shifts so I have no idea if any of them would know who you're even talking about. You have no idea how many people we see and serve on a daily basis - let alone weeks or months ago. As you know, it's like a revolving door around here, from those we serve to those who work here and all of the rest of the staff. Even the medical professionals, unless there's information on someone needing treatment, all documents and information are strictly confidential. By law we can't release any information or we could be held liable. Take care." She headed back to her desk.

*****

The streets were dying down as Vicky headed back across to the other side of town, her mind raging in a hundred different directions as she tried to console herself that she wasn't crazy though her subconscious begged to differ. The concierge was empty as she entered the lobby and headed toward the elevators up to her lavish condominium and entered the spacious unit then collapsed on the couch. It had been one excruciatingly long day, she dropped her head and weeped for awhile.

There was no way she would ever be able to wrap her mind around any of it. *And who would ever believe it, for that matter?* She rationalized. *They would say she was crazy for sure... and once again...maybe they were right...* she bargained with herself, then stepped back outside into the soft pitter-patter of the gentle evening showers cleansing the earth as a tiny piece of paper caught her eye.

Quickly reaching down to retrieve it, she skimmed over the mysterious weathered piece of parchment and examined the ancient document in courier font, curious where it had come from.

"Angel sightings have been reported since the beginning of time
- yet no one can prove them. Only the accounts and recollections of mankind
and the recollections of those often in times of warfare when subjects may feel alone and under duress
or in a state of euphoria."

Anonymous

Vicky leaned over the balcony and looked across the empty lot into the evening glare of the motel lights, once again reminiscing on the night before. In her heart of hearts, she had always known that it was Ralph, a shiver tingled down her spine as she clutched the vintage article to her chest and said a silent prayer...

The End

*"He that dwelleth in the secret place
of the most high
shall abide under the shadow
of the Almighty.
I will say of the LORD,
He is my refuge
and my fortress: my God;
in him will I trust."
Psalm 91:1-2*

www.ingramcontent.com/pod-product-compliance
Lightning Source LLC
LaVergne TN
LVHW021236080526
838199LV00088B/4536